LOVE LESSONS

NIKKI BROWN

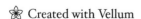

THANK YOU!

I would like to thank each and every one of you for rocking
with me the way you do. There are no words to accurately
describe what that means to me. Thank you! Thank you!
Thank you! From the bottom of my heart!

ALSO BY NIKKI BROWN

FOLLOW ME

Follow me on social media
Facebook: Author Nikki Brown
Facebook Reading Group: Nikki's Haven
Instagram: @nikkibrown_theauthor
Twitter: @NikkiBrownSWP
www.authornikkibrown.com

Text Nikki to 66866 to join my mailing list

Chapter One

LESSON 1

Love Has No Room For Jealousy

"Maybe he just forgot, Navi. You know he's been super busy at work and shit like that." Nixie attempted to convince her sister that her boyfriend of three years didn't purposely miss one of the most important days of her life.

However, this wasn't the first time that he had left Nixie hanging. Navi sensed the pattern far before Nixie even gave it a second thought, which prompted conversations like this often. Adam wasn't as dedicated to their relationship, and the only person that couldn't see that was Nixie.

"Nix, I love you, but you got to stop making excuses for him." Navi sighed and rolled her eyes as if her sister could see her, while Nixie, on the other end of the phone, was massaging her temples in an attempt to soothe the headache that was threatening to strike. "And stop rubbing ya damn temples like I'm getting on ya nerves."

Nixie giggled and shook her head. She and her sister were the best of friends; they knew each other like the backs of their hands.

"When you stop rolling your got damn eyes, I'll stop rubbing my temples."

"You don't know me, Nix."

"So you ain't just roll your eyes again?" Nixie balanced the phone between her ear and shoulder as she waited for her sister to answer. When all she heard was light giggles, she knew that she was right.

"Whatever. But stop trying to change the subject. That man does not deserve you. You are beautiful, talented, and overall, too good of a woman for him. Today should have shown you just how much he cares about you and what you have going on," Navi fussed.

Nixie was just like their mother, too forgiving and too understanding, in her opinion. They watched their mother take so much shit from their father until, eventually, he just left all together. Navi learned from that, but from the looks of it, her sister had some of their mother's tendencies.

"Navi, you just don't like Adam. He's not that bad. Sometimes he just puts work before everything, including me."

"And that's not a problem for you, Nixie?" Her high-pitched tone soared through the phone, making Nixie pull the phone away from her ear to relieve the ringing of her eardrum. "I'm a business owner, just like you. I know what it means to lose track of time with your shit, but at the end of the day, I make sure to make my husband, who I love, a priority."

"I am a priority in Adam's life." The confidence trailed off in her tone just like her words did, and Navi didn't miss it.

"Hoe, he doesn't even support your fucking business. When was the last time he used any of your products?" Navi paused for theatrics because she knew her sister would never answer her. "Exactly! I mean, let's be serious; he's jealous because he knows your potential. He knows that you can do anything you put your mind to, including leaving his sorry ass."

"I love you, sister, and I'm about to lay down." Nixie yawned for emphasis.

She didn't want to argue with her sister, and she damn sure didn't want to let her know that she had been feeling the exact same way for a while now. Nixie knew firsthand what happened when you put your family in your business, so she opted to keep that to herself. So instead of adding fuel to the fire, she thought it was best to just put it out.

"Umph! Well since you cutting me off, I expect payment for my services to be in the form of lunch at Chima's." Navi hung up the phone without giving Nixie a chance to respond.

"This bitch." Nixie chuckled while pressing the message icon on her phone. She typed a message to her sister and hit send.

Bitch don't be hanging up on me 😒

Nixie didn't even get her phone on her lap good before her phone dinged, signaling that Navi had texted her back.

Respect yo elders hoe 👆

Sighing, Nixie pulled herself from the sofa and headed upstairs to the bathroom in her home, to prepare to turn down for the night. Today had been an amazing day for her, despite Adam not showing up. She couldn't believe that her pop-up shop was such a success. Never in a million years did she think that something she whipped up in her kitchen for her own bad skin, would turn into a money-making career.

Nix Beauty was started two years ago when she was having trouble with her skin care and couldn't figure out how to control her eczema. Her skin was extremely sensitive. Even the medicine the doctors prescribed affected her.

Tired of the up and down with her eczema, Nixie ended up watching a tutorial of a woman creating her own all-natural skin care line, and that was all it took.

On a mission, Nixie did her research and tried out different products on her own skin until she came up with a perfect all-natural blend, and within months, she was able to share it with her family and friends. It didn't take long for word to get out, and with the help of social media, she was now shipping all over the US.

The door chiming pulled her from her thoughts as she slowly massaged her temples and waited for *him* to find his way up the stairs. The minute she saw his face, a frown etched its way onto hers as she waited for him to address her. When he didn't, she scoffed and placed her hands on her hips, trying her best not to fall victim to his sexiness like she had so many times before.

"And where the fuck were you?" Her tone was soft and calm, but the fire in her eyes was anything but.

She hated herself in that moment for still being *physically* attracted to him. Her heart was hurt, her mind wanted to stab him a hundred times, but her damn lady parts were leaking due to the smell of his enticing cologne.

Sexy muthafucka!

Adam was fine; not your ordinary boy next door fine, but the take all of your clothes off and throw your ass at him fine. The problem was he knew it.

He wasn't extremely tall, standing at five feet eleven, give or take an inch. His skin was like the color of peanut butter, with a set of sneaky, light brown eyes to match. He had hair the color of sand that gave him a pretty boy look, but his bad boy demeanor contradicted that. He was sexy, and there was no doubt about it.

"You would think all that Ivy League schooling would have taught you not to speak in such a derogatory manner," he countered as he slowly peeled off his navy-blue blazer, bringing her gaze to the way the crisp white shirt laid against his chiseled chest.

Adam glanced over at his girlfriend of three years and shook his head. He attempted to prepare himself for the argument that he was going to be walking into, but there was no preparing when Nixie was pissed, so he did the next best thing: he deflected.

"Where I did and did not go to school has nothing to do with the fact that you missed one of the most important days of my life. What kind of shit is that?" Her tone didn't escalate, and her facial expression didn't falter. She was sick of him acting like she should apologize for how she grew up. If he only knew that her life growing up was far from perfect.

"I had to work, Nixie. You know, walk into a building and clock in and actually do something." He released an aggravated chuckle. Things were so much better between the two of them when she worked a regular nine to five. Now that she was on her *be your own boss* bullshit, she didn't take into consideration that others still had to punch a clock, and that aggravated him.

Adam was exhausted. He hadn't had the best of days, so an argument wasn't what he was looking for, but when Nixie scoffed, he knew that this conversation was about to take a turn for the worst.

"You act like that shit is my fault!" And there it went; the calm demeanor was out the window, and the pissed off Nixie was in full effect. "I'm sorry I worked my ass off to build a brand that allows me to work from home. I tried to get you to start your own real estate firm. *However,* you would rather *walk into a building and clock in and actually do something,*" she mocked, throwing his words back at him.

"I'm not about to sit here and argue with you. I had a long day at work, and I just wanted to come home, have a beer, and watch fucking SportsCenter, and I can't even fucking do that."

Adam snatched the tie that was around his neck off and threw it to the ground before his eyes found hers. He was trying to think of when their relationship had gone downhill, but he couldn't pinpoint it. What he did know was that he was the cause of it; he just didn't know where to begin to fix it.

He sighed when he saw the lone tear fall down her cheek.

Nixie was kicking herself for allowing even one tear to fall. She hated to cry and rarely ever did. Her feelings really had to be hurt for her to allow her liquid emotions to roam free. Crying made her feel weak, and she was anything but.

"My day was amazing! I was so thankful for my sister, mom, and stepdad for showing up for me because if I had to depend on your ass, I would have been up shit's creek without a fucking paddle." She shook her head and wiped the few tears that forced their way out. "I sold out within the first two hours. I'm so got damn proud of myself, regardless of who else is." Her brows hitched as she turned to walk off.

Once she was in the bathroom, she slammed the door and turned the shower water on. Placing her hands on the counter, she hung her head down and thought about the words that her sister said.

He's jealous of you... He doesn't deserve you.

Her heart started to pound in her chest, and her breathing picked up. The feeling she felt was foreign, and she didn't like it. She took her hand and wiped the steam off the mirror and stared at herself.

"You are an amazing woman! You're a fucking boss, and you need to get your shit together!" She coached herself. Her eyes danced around her slim thick frame as she took in her beautiful features that came straight from her mama.

Her naturally curly hair framed her beautiful face and fell right below her jawline. Her doe shaped eyes were an exact replica of her mother and sisters. It made them look exotic and alluring. Nixie had the body of a dancer—long legs, toned thighs, and a nonexistent stomach. Her breasts were a solid C-cup, and her ass was perfectly round. She was beautiful inside and out and deserved none of what Adam was offering her at the moment.

Taking a deep breath, she smiled in the mirror and nodded. She wasn't about to let him or anyone else take away her joy on today. Her business hit another milestone, and now more than ever, she was confident to move on to the next phase.

Adam stood on the other side of the door listening to her talk to herself in the mirror. He hated when she did that. It made him feel like she was gearing herself up to leave him. Nixie was a prize in every sense of the word, and he was dropping the ball big time. He just didn't know how to stop himself.

Damage control in affect! he thought as he slowly pulled the door open. Steam instantly slapped him in the face, causing him to have to take in a few sharp breaths. He never could understand how she could shower in water that hot. It was the main reason why they never showered together.

"Look, I'm sorry. Today was a rough day for me. The company is downsizing and making a bunch of changes. Some jobs may be at risk. Even with all of that, I shouldn't have taken my frustrations out on you. I just didn't think me being there was a big deal since this is your *thing*."

"You're missing the point! You were supposed to fucking be there, Adam. You told me that you would, and you didn't keep your word, per usual!" She rolled her eyes and continued enjoying the feel of the hot water beating down on her sore muscles.

"Why did you want me there so bad, Nixie? To do what? Take money? Restock your table, what?"

She slowly turned his way with her brows knitted and lips pursed.

"I didn't *want* you there. I *needed* you there. Why the fuck can't you see that, Adam? Then again, why do I expect you to." She chuckled, but there was nothing humorous about it. "If it's not about Adam Leary, you don't give a fuck."

"You know that's not true. I have a job to do, Nixie, whether you like it or not. That's the reality of it. I just didn't have the time to be your cheerleader!" His tone raised a few octaves higher than Nixie was willing to deal with, further pissing her off.

"You make time for what you want to, Adam. I guarantee you if it was an important dinner or party and you needed me to be your *cheerleader*, you would expect me to be there! If I didn't show up because I had to *work*, you wouldn't be okay with it, and neither am I!" she said with finality.

Adam mumbled under his breath as he glared at her through the glass shower door. He wanted to say so much more, but he knew it would get him nowhere. He hated how he felt when it came to Nixie's sudden success. Truth of the matter was, she intimidated him; she always had. She was the first woman he had ever been with that had something going for herself. He always stayed away from women like that for his own selfish reasons.

The more successful she became, the less of a man he felt like, and that made him resent her in a sense. What Adam didn't know was that his insecurities were pushing her away.

"I'm sorry, Nix."

"You can leave, Adam," was all she said.

As far as she was concerned, the conversation was over, and she didn't have anything else to say to him. This conversation was an ongoing thing, and she was exhausted. It wasn't that hard to understand that you were supposed to support your partner, and Nixie was done trying to explain it. From now on, she was going to give him exactly what he gave her, *nothing!*

"You're just like your fucking mama." He thought he mumbled, but she heard him loud and clear, and he was sure of it when his eyes met hers.

"I bet you won't say that shit to her." She seethed as he shook his head and turned to leave the bathroom.

Once the door was shut, Nixie knew right then and there that if things didn't change and fast that she would be closing the page on this chapter in her life.

Chapter Two

LESSON 2

Love Isn't Enough

"Yo, I need a favor, bro." Kawan casually strolled into Airy's office as if his name was plastered on the front door.

A lopsided grin spread across Airy's face as he looked at his friend and colleague.

"Learning how to fucking knock wasn't included in your school, huh?"

"Fuck you and knocking, how about that shit." Kawan chuckled and slid himself into the chair that was parallel to the one that Airy was sitting in. "Like I was saying, I need a favor big time."

Airy Menz was one of the top commercial real estate agents at Queen City Realty. The fact that his father owned the company had nothing to do with his success. He made sure that he was on the top of every sales board at every meeting. Airy made sure to always be the first one to work and the last one to leave. He was a hustler at heart, just like his father. The street life that led him there helped with that as well.

He met Kawan when he was hired as a mortgage broker over six years ago. The two clicked instantly, and Airy ended up talking Kawan into taking the real estate exam and even helped him study for it. Once he passed, Airy made sure that he showed him the ropes, and he soared through the company quickly.

"Tell me what you want so I can tell your ass no." A chuckle vibrated through his chest, bringing his eyes to his friend. Airy shrugged when Kawan threw him a bird. "Real shit, the fuck you want?"

"My mother-in-law thinks I'm Superman, and she needs me to show my sister-in-law a few properties for her store that she's trying to open up. Well I told them to come by tomorrow, and Charles just called about his new building downtown. He's ready to put it on the market. Tomorrow is the only time he has available." Kawan looked away and then settled on his friend again.

"You beating 'round the bush, and it's aggravating me." Airy chuckled. "You know how I feel about that. I don't have patience for shit."

"Calm your hyper ass down. I need you to show her a few things tomorrow."

"How you know I didn't have shit to do?"

"Nigga, because our fucking calendars are linked." Kawan

leaned back in the high back chair that he was occupying, crossed his arms across his chest, and smirked.

Kawan already knew that he would do it, so he was already sending over the properties that Nixie had picked out that she wanted to see and a few that he wanted her to see. He just didn't have the time to actually do it himself.

"Who getting the commission off this?" Airy's brows hitched as he fought against the smile that was tugging at his lips.

"We can split it." Kawan shrugged before he burst out laughing.

"Nah, that's a no-go, nigga, straight up."

"I did all the work already; you just gotta show up." Kawan smirked.

He was fucking with Airy. He would never take money out of his pockets, especially since he was doing him a huge favor.

"What kind of business is it, because I just got a few new properties in that I haven't even listed yet."

"She makes and sales all-natural beauty products, and she's an esthetician. So, she'll need a place to make, store, and sell her products, as well as work with clients."

"I got the perfect property." Airy typed away on his computer until he pulled up what he was looking for. "I was actually in the process of getting this loaded into the system, but now I think I'll wait. I'll show this one first, that way if she don't want it, then I can put it on the site ASAP. I think she's gonna fall in love though." He turned his MacBook around so that Kawan could take a look at the property.

"Is this next door? What happened to the little spa that used to be there?"

"They went out of business. I went and looked at the property yesterday, and the shit is nice. I was excited to put it on the market, but I'm sure your sister-in-law is gonna snatch it up."

"I think she gon' love it, and it's near her sister's boutique. You know Navi is on the other side of the strip mall that's directly beside this one."

"Even better." Airy smiled and rubbed his hands together, excited for the opportunity to make some quick money.

"Keep it professional too, nigga." Kawan stood, pointing at Airy.

"I'm always professional." The smirk on Airy's face caused him to shake his head.

"Like Constance Mirelle professional."

The smirk faded from his face as his eyes narrowed at Kawan. He hated to hear that name, let alone think of just how big of a mistake she was. Constance was Airy's headache, and the fact that she wasn't giving up so easily was making things just as hard.

"That's fucked up."

"I'm just saying, Airy. Nixie is beautiful, and she's your type." Kawan's brows dipped in. "You've even said it when you came to our Christmas party last year."

Airy looked up in the sky as he folded his arms across his chest. He was trying to think back to the party that he was talking about. They hung out all the time, and he had met his wife Navi a few times, but he couldn't remember her sister.

"I don't think I remember."

"She looks just like Navi but she's a little... thicker around back, if you know what I'm saying." Kawan felt awkward saying it, but it was the truth. It was the one thing that separated the two, other than Navi wearing her hair in huge curls all over her head that hung past her shoulders and Nixie wearing hers cut shorter, framing her round face with a ton of the same curls.

"Ahh, she was the one who had your wife at your neck the whole night." The two shared a look and Kawan grumbled bringing a low chortle from Adam.

Airy remembered her walking around with a frown on her face the whole night. Going back and forth between pretending to have a good time and arguing with someone on the phone. He only noticed because whoever she was arguing with seemed to upset Navi, which in turn aggravated Kawan.

"Yeah she's fucking with Adam down in finance." Kawan's eyes rolled over the amused look on Airy's face. "Dude didn't show up and had her on some other shit."

"That short nigga?"

"Yeah man." Kawan's laugh filled the room. "So just keep it professional because I know how you are, Airy. Nixie and Navi are super close, and a nigga ain't trying to be paying for your fuck ups."

"Ye of so little faith." All thirty-two of his teeth were now on display. Airy had a way with the ladies; he wouldn't profess himself as a ladies' man, but the ladies did love him.

"Yo, whatever. Don't make me fuck you up, Airy."

"What time tomorrow?" He waved Kawan off and turned to his computer. He wanted to say more to fuck with him, but he decided to let him live.

"I told them to come at three."

"Cool. That works for me."

"Good looking out, bruh."

"Kawan, take all that sappy shit out of here. You know if don't no one got you, I do."

"I already know."

———

Nixie had in her Beats Pro headphones with some old Keyshia Cole playing as she danced around the kitchen. Today was the day that she hoped to finally get the ball moving on her storefront. She was excited and nervous at the same time, but she knew this was the move that she was set to make.

"I stayed around thinking you would learn to love." Nixie sang as she rolled her hips while taking the couple pieces of bacon that she had cooked out of the pan and placed them on her plate. "I shoulda let you go." She continued to sing "Shoulda Let You Go" by Keyshia Cole.

Once everything was done, she walked over to the break-fast nook and pressed pause on her phone and bowed her head. After saying a quick prayer, she turned the music back on and dug into her food.

Nixie scrolled through social media, stopping at a picture of her sister and brother-in-law. She couldn't help the smile that tugged at her lips. Navi and Kawan were couple goals in her eyes, and she couldn't wait until she got to experience what they had. Their relationship wasn't perfect, but they were perfect for each other.

She knew that she didn't have that with Adam. In fact, Adam was starting to remind her more and more of the man that she had grown to hate, the same man that went half on creating her being. Nixie had been wasting her time with Adam, and his actions were proving that by the day.

"Good morning." Adam's deep voice carried its way through the mid-size kitchen.

He stopped in his tracks when his salutation wasn't reciprocated. Adam took in a sharp breath before turning around to see that Nixie had headphones in. Walking in her direction, he leaned down over the breakfast nook so that he was eye level with her. When her gaze fell on him, she offered up a smile. It wasn't genuine, but it was all she had to offer at the moment.

Pressing pause on her phone, she gave him her attention. He chuckled at the fact that she didn't bother to remove the headphones, letting him know that she was still pissed from the night before. Sighing, he leaned in and kissed her lips which also wasn't reciprocated.

"Good morning, Nixie."

"Morning."

"How'd you sleep?"

"Great." Her answers were short and to the point.

"Really, because I tossed and turned all night in the bed by myself." His brows knitted in as he waited on her to address what he had just said.

After their fight the previous night, Nixie thought it was best that he slept in the guest room. She didn't want to be anywhere near him. He thought she was taking her attitude a little overboard, and she felt he wasn't taking it serious enough. Adam didn't fight her on it though. As bad as he didn't want to, he grabbed his pillow and headed for the guest room where he didn't get any sleep.

"Sorry." She smirked as she hit play on her phone and began bobbing her head to her music while she finished what was left of her breakfast.

Her curly hair was parted on the side with one side slicked back and the other falling in her face. Big hoop earrings hung from her ear, and she wore light makeup and gloss on her lips. She was beautiful, even when she was pissed.

Adam opened his mouth to tell her so but decided against it. Turning, he walked into the kitchen, went to the cabinet, and grabbed him a plate. When he walked to the stove, grabbing the handle, he looked inside. *Nothing!* He opened the microwave, and it was empty too. That's when he realized that there was no food for him.

"You have got to be shitting me."

He closed his eyes and counted backwards from ten. His

anger was rising, and he didn't want to fight before he went in to work. On top of the fact he tended to say things that he didn't mean when he was angry, he was trying to get himself in check. Chuckling inwardly, he stepped in front of Nixie and took the headphones out of her ears.

Her eyes slowly rose to where he was standing and then focused in on her earphones that were in his hands, before lifting to meet his evil glare.

"Can I have those back?" Her attitude was peaking, and she didn't have any interest in stopping it. She was annoyed, and him interrupting her chill time pissed her off.

"Did you not fix me any breakfast?"

"Nope."

Nixie snorted as she looked him up and down. It was the first time in a while that her irritation with him overpowered her attraction to him. She gave a silent thank you to her core for not defying her yet again.

"And why the hell not?" he asked through clenched teeth.

"Simple." She tilted her head to the side and crossed her arms across her chest. "You weren't there for me when I needed you, so I was returning the favor." Adam couldn't even boil water. He depended solely on Nixie to eat if he wasn't eating out. She knew that, which was why she did what she did, and she was loving his reaction.

Now he knows how the fuck I feel!

"That's petty fucking bullshit, and you know it. You not cooking for me has nothing to do with the fact that I couldn't show up to help you yesterday."

"It has everything to do with it. It's fucking crazy to me how you don't get that." Nixie shook her head as she slid the last piece of bacon into her mouth and chewed very slowly.

Now that was petty, asshole!

"What don't I get, Nix? Please tell me because right now, you're acting like I fucked another bitch in our bed or something. Got damn! I missed one little event, and you're acting like I did something so fucking wrong."

"That *little* event meant the world to me, and if you can't see that, then fuck you, Adam. Don't worry about me or my *little* events anymore. I got me! Know that!"

"Wow! Just wow! I can't believe you—"

"Save it." She stood up and headed to the door where someone was knocking. When she pulled it opened, Adam knew that his day had just gone from bad to worse in a matter of minutes. "Let me get my keys and purse from upstairs," Nixie told her sister.

"Ewww, why you looking like that? Today is an amazing day. You're about to embark on your dreams and pave the way for your legacy. Put a damn smile on ya face, hoe, and let's go make history." Navi clapped her hands in her sister's direction.

"I would hardly call making soap, making history," Adam mumbled.

"Yeah, well I hardly call a selfish, non-supportive daddy's boy, a man either." Navi cut her eyes at Adam before she cocked her head, daring him to say something. "But I guess we all got our own way of thinking, huh?"

Adam grumbled and turned to head up the stairs after Nixie. "Nix, can we talk?"

"Nope. I got shit to do."

Nixie heard exactly what he had just said about her making soap wasn't making history, but she chose not to respond. What he wanted from her was a reaction, and he didn't deserve her energy or her time.

After realizing that she wasn't slowing down to converse with him, Adam stepped in her path; grabbing her arm and pulling her to him, he sighed. When she snatched away and got in his face, he put his hands up in surrender and backed away.

"I just don't want to go all day with you pissed at me." Running his hands down his face, he focused on the ground for a second before returning his pleading glare.

"Yeah, well I don't want to live my life unhappy, so I guess we both got some shit to think about, huh?"

Adam shook his head at how much she sounded like her mother and sister. They all had smart mouths and overpowering attitudes, and he hated it. Women were supposed to be meek and submissive. They were supposed to let the man be the man. His father always drilled that in his head and heart. Nixie wasn't anything like the women his father told him about. That was the very thing that he loved and hated about her at the same time.

"Nix, will you just—"

"Haven't you fucked up my day enough? You've successfully ruined yet another important day of my life. The least you can do is let me leave without one of your bullshit ass apologies."

"Nix—"

"Adam!"

"Okay, okay." He threw his hands up and took a step back. "We can talk about this when I get off."

"Nah, I don't want to talk about this at all, Adam. The conversation is getting kind of old, don't you think?" Her right brow lifted.

Adam was just digging himself deeper and deeper in that same hole, and if he kept it up, there would be no escape. Once he realized the damage he had done, he reached out for her, but she was already halfway down the stairs.

"Fuck!"

When Nixie got to the bottom of the stairs, she was on the brink of tears. Her heart was hurt. Even though she knew in her heart he wasn't the man for her, she still loved him. She just didn't think she could keep ignoring the way he treated her.

One look at her sister's face had Navi ready to commit the ultimate sin. "Oh, he about to fight me, and I'm calling Ma," Navi said as she marched toward the stairs. "He got you and me fucked up!"

"Navi, let's just go. I just need to go!"

"After I—"

"Navi!"

"Fine, but I'm still calling Ma. I don't care what you say. Let's go before I set this damn house on fire with his ass in it," Navi said loud enough for Adam to hear, but he knew not to say anything.

"You can't do that, because it's in my name." Nixie rolled her eyes as she shut the door behind her and turned to lock it.

Navi scoffed and walked out to the car, hopping into the driver's seat. She was pissed, and it was time for her sister to wake up and realize that Adam was not the man for her. Even if she had to shake some sense into her, shit needed to change and fast.

Nixie already knew how the ride down to Queen City Realty was about to be. So, the minute her ass was in the seat, her fingers were on her temples, drawing an eye roll from Navi.

"Nix, you know how I feel about Adam, but why? Why do you put up with that?"

"I still love him, Navi."

Sighing heavily, she peered over at her sister. "Baby, sometimes love ain't enough."

The words danced around Nixie's mind, and she thought about how things had changed so drastically within the past year and a half with her and Adam. It was true she loved him, but she fell out of love with him long ago.

"I know."

"What do you mean you know?"

"I—I just didn't want to get y'all involved. Shit with me and Adam hasn't been the best in a while. Shit just got too comfortable for the both of us. He's convenient right now." She tugged on a curl that had fallen forward. "I've never seen a future with him. I just let this shit go longer than I should have."

Saying that out loud caused a lump to form in her throat, and before she could stop them, the tears decorated her cheeks. Nixie bit down on her back teeth to stop the sob that was trying to force its way out, to no avail.

"Baby, don't cry." Navi reached over and grabbed her sister's hands. "I didn't mean to make you upset, but I be damn if I let you follow in mom's footsteps and sit back and do nothing. Hell, you were there. You know what she went through and for eighteen whole years until he up and left her for that bitch. She did that shit because she was comfortable. I don't want that to be you."

Maybe I am like my mother.

"I didn't realize things were this bad until yesterday. Then I was like, okay, bitch; you know better." Nixie wiped her eyes with the back of her hands. "I'm done though. He wants a woman who's not college educated but proper and prim, who doesn't have goals but makes a lot of money. The nigga is a walking contradiction."

Navi snapped her head at her sister, and they both burst out laughing. Nixie didn't realize just how much she needed this moment with her sister until then. That's why she loved her family; it only consisted of her sister, mom, brother-in-law, and stepdad, but that was all she needed.

"You stupid as hell." Navi shook her head. "In all serious-ness, if he don't make you happy anymore, leave him. Love takes work, Nix, and if he ain't willing to roll up his sleeves and get dirty with you, then he ain't the one for you. Like I said, sometimes love ain't enough."

"You right." Nixie nodded her head.

"Aight, girl, we here. You ready to make this happen?" Navi parked the car and laid her head against the headrest and looked over at her sister.

"Hell yeah." The two high-fived and peeled themselves out of the car and headed into the building.

Chapter Three

LESSON 3

Love Has Empathy

A iry looked down at his ringing phone. He smiled when he saw that it was his mother. He hadn't talked to her in over two weeks. She and his father had just come back from vacation, and he had been swamped with work, so hearing her voice would surely put him in a better mood.

"Hey, my lady."

"Don't you hey me. That woman been by here again. I thought I told you to tell that hussy to stay away from my house before I deck her in the eye. You must have thought I was playing," she fussed.

Airy groaned and pulled the phone away from his ear. He didn't understand what his ex, Constance, didn't understand about them being over. It was aggravating for him, especially when he wasn't the cause of their relationship's demise.

"I'll handle it, Ma."

"You said that last time, Airy Montez Menz." He cringed, hearing her call him by his government name. He never connected with his middle name, and she was the only person that called him that, especially when she was pissed off at him. "If I have to do it, you're going to be bailing me out again."

A throaty rumble escaped his lips as he shook his head at the memory. It was right after he had broken up with Constance and she tried to break the windows out of his house. His mother pulled up just in time to catch her and deliver an old fashion ass whipping.

"Where Pops at?"

"Why? You think I care about what he got to say? He knows who he married, and that's why he lets me do what I got to do and love me afterwards. When you love someone, you don't try and change them, Airy."

His mother's words echoed in his head, but his attention was somewhere else. His mouth hung open as he went to say something to his mother, but no words came out. Airy's eyes traveled from her freshly painted toes up to the host of curls that hovered over to one side of her head.

"Damn!" Lust was thick and laced in every syllable that left his lips.

"Boy, I know you ain't cussing me," Anna said through the phone, bringing Airy's thoughts back to their conversation.

"Ma, let me call you back. I think I just met your daughter-in-law." He hung up with her fussing in his ear, but he didn't have time to explain. "Wow!" slipped his lips.

His eyes narrowed in on the thin belly chain that held a single diamond that hung delicately in her belly button. That one little detail had his dick bricking up in his slacks. The woman before him was sexy beyond measures.

The black linen, wide legged pants that she wore hung slightly off of her hips, bringing his attention to her womanly curves. His tongue slid across his lips as he imagined holding her up by her waist and bringing her down on his manhood then—

"Ah hell," Navi said, waving her hand in the air. "Are you Airy?"

Airy's eyes never left Nixie's as she undressed every inch of him in her mind. She thought Adam was sexy; he had nothing on the chocolate God that now stood before her. Tucking her bottom lip between her teeth, she fought against the seductive smile that was tugging at her lips.

"Professional, nigga." Kawan seemed to appear out of nowhere and entered his office with a glare on his face. "Where's Ma?" He walked around and stood directly in front of Nixie with his back to Airy, drawing a chuckle from him.

"Stan was sick, and you know how she is when her man is sick." Nixie spoke for the first time, and her singsong tone had him ready to get down on one knee and propose right there.

"How are you when *your man* is sick?" Airy peeked his head around Kawan's broad frame.

"Nigga." Kawan dropped his head and shook it before his

eyes met his wife who had a silly smirk on his face. "Come on, baby, not you too. You supposed to be on my side."

Everyone chuckled but Kawan. He threw an evil glare over his shoulders. Airy's eyes were back on Nixie. Nothing that Kawan was saying was registering with him. *She* had every ounce of attention that he had to give, and she accepted it with open arms.

"I don't really like my man right now, so I would sit and watch him suffer." Nixie giggled and looked over at Navi who urged her to move closer.

"I'll be back, sis. I'ma go and talk to Kawan for a minute."

"Kawan, what happened to Mr. Charles?" Airy asked, wondering what happened to the appointment that he originally had. Not that he was complaining because being in Nixie's presence had him ready to do things he thought he would never do.

"He rescheduled at the last minute. That's what I was coming in here to tell you, that I could take them so you can do what you need to do," Kawan said as he grabbed Navi and Nixie's hand to walk them out of the office, but Airy stopped him before he could.

"That's okay, Ms. Land..." His words trailed off as he focused in on her ass and nodded in approval. "She has me for the rest of the day."

"Airy, mannnnn." Kawan shook his head.

"We good, bro. You're more than welcome to join us." Airy shrugged. He didn't care how, but he wanted to be in Nixie's presence, even if a permanent cock blocker was going to be front and center. His heart and body were pulling him to her, and he didn't want to disappoint either.

He remembered her from the Christmas party, but he didn't remember her looking that damn good. Then again, it could have been because he was with Constance, and he didn't really pay that much attention to her, but right now, he *saw* her.

"No! Actually, we're gonna go home and spend some quality time together." Navi looked up at her husband as she dragged her nail down the center of his shirt, being sure to hit each button on the way down. "It's much needed, don't you think?" She winked.

Kawan bit his lip, looking down at his wife. She had his dick rising, and he was pissed because now nothing was going to stop him from taking her home and giving her what she wanted. Not even the fact that it was led by her eagerness to get Nixie and Airy alone.

Groaning, he leaned down and kissed his wife before turning his skeptical gaze to Airy, who hadn't stopped looking at Nixie since she got there.

"Airy, take care of my sister, man."

"I got her, like I told you. She's going to love the first building that I show her. I gotta feeling that I know her style."

"Keep your got damn hands to yourself," Kawan warned, drawing a chuckle from Airy.

"I'll be the perfect gentleman."

"Call me when you ready for me to pick you up," Navi said with the same goofy smirk as before.

"No worries. I'll be glad to *take her home.*"

"Y'all go out in the hallway. Let me holla at my boy real quick," Kawan said between clenched teeth.

Navi and Nixie laughed and made their way into the hall-way, leaving the two men alone. The two could hear them going back and forth, causing them to break into laughter. They were laughing so hard that they didn't even realize they had company.

"What are you doing here, Nix?" Adam asked, finally taking in her appearance. He hated when she dressed like a hippie, and the last thing he needed was for someone to see her with him, like that. "And why are you dressed like that?"

"You really want your ass beat, bruh," Navi said, taking a step forward, but Nixie stepped in front of her to stop her. "I got time today."

Out of the two, Navi was definitely the firecracker. Nixie had her days too, but Navi wasn't down for anyone's bullshit. She had learned from her mother's mistakes, and trust wasn't something that came easy with her.

"I'm going to look at buildings today. I'm not here to see you. I thought you worked on the first floor; I didn't even think we would run into each other." She rolled her eyes and adjusted the strap on her purse. "And my clothes are fine."

"It's a sexy ass man on the other side of that door who likes the hell out of them," Navi mumbled. Nixie cleared her throat and ran her hands through her curly hair to redirect the nervous energy that had just shot through her body.

"What did you just say?" Adam asked.

"I said—"

"Nothing, she said nothing." Nixie's brows knitted in. "Chill, Navi."

"I'm just saying, the nigga needs to wake up." She raised her brows and tilted her head.

Adam looked back and forth from the sisters. Their relationship irked him, more so because he was an only child, and he didn't get the pleasure of growing up with a best friend. It was like he wasn't dating just Nixie; he had to please her mom and sister too, and that was something he couldn't get with. That and the fact they often made him feel like he was a stranger on the outside looking in.

"Why didn't you just ask me? I could have hooked you up with a realtor and got you financed. All you had to do was ask."

Nixie scoffed. "Are you serious right now?" She shook her head and turned to walk off, but he grabbed her arm to stop her. When she snatched away, Navi stepped in front of her. This was what he didn't like. What they were going through had nothing to do with her, but here she was, front and center, ready to fight her sister's battles.

"Navi, no disrespect, but this ain't got shit to do with you. Maybe if you mind your business, things with us wouldn't be so bad."

"Excuse you!" Navi screeched.

"What's going on with you and me had nothing to do with my sister, but you being a narcissistic, inconsiderate asshole has everything to do with it. I shouldn't have to *ask* you a got damn thing when you see me out here working my ass off. If you paid attention to me and my needs instead of always focusing on your own, you would know! That shit should be a given." Nixie dropped her head and sighed before her loaded gaze found Adam again. "A man who gave a fuck would have been ready and willing. The fact that you feel like I had to ask you tells me a lot."

"I'm not a fucking mind reader, Nix. How in the hell was I supposed to know that you wanted my help?"

"You ready, beautiful?" Airy seemed to float through the door, inserting himself directly between Nixie and Adam. "I'm *ready* and *willing* to take you to see the property that I found. I ain't even put it on the market yet. You get first dibs." Airy smiled down at Nixie.

She wasn't too short, maybe around five feet six, but Airy's tall frame towered over hers immensely. Looking up at him, she got lost in his brown eyes, and for a second, she forgot where she was and that her boyfriend was standing a few feet away.

Clearing her throat again, she smiled and nodded her head. "I would love that. I'm outgrowing my kitchen, and I need somewhere to get stuff done. I eventually want to expand my business internationally."

"And you do all-natural soaps, right?" Nixie nodded while moving a curl that had fallen down in her eyes. Airy wanted to take a hand full of her curly tresses and tilt her head back and shove his tongue down her throat, but he refrained. "I bet they work wonders for dry skin, huh?" He nodded, turning his attention to Adam. "Alex, right?" He purposely said the wrong name.

"Adam. Nixie, can I talk to you for a second?"

"You use her products, right?" Airy ignored his attempt to get Nixie's attention.

She wasn't his. He had barely had a conversation with her, but he felt the need to protect her. Something about Adam's presence made Nixie sad. It was like he could feel it, and for some odd reason, that made him sad, and he didn't like it at all.

"So how far is the first building?" The silent awkwardness had Nixie feeling uneasy. She was pissed at Adam, and she felt like maybe their relationship had run its course, but she wasn't about to play him in front of a complete stranger, no matter how fine the said stranger was.

"It's literally right next door."

"Nix, you'll be right around the corner from me!" Navi squealed. "Babe, I changed my mind. I want to see this building."

"Navi, I thought you said—" Kawan started, but Navi stood on her tiptoes and whispered in his ear.

"Trust me, waiting will be worth it for you." She kissed the side of his face and made him clear his throat. "Y'all ready?" She looked at her husband, Airy, and then her sister, purposely ignoring the look that Adam was giving.

"Ye-yeah, let's go." Nixie turned to walk off, but Adam grabbed her again.

This time instead of it being Navi, he had both Airy and Kawan in his face, ready to go to war. Nixie jumped in between them, placing her hand on Airy's chest and Kawan's shoulders. That simple gesture infuriated Adam, but he knew not to make a move.

Kawan didn't care for him, and the feeling was mutual. That was a family matter. When it came to Airy, going up against him would cost him his job, and he couldn't have that.

"Nixie, can you please just talk to me for a second?"

Her eyes met Airy's, and he was silently praying for her not to go. He couldn't explain why he didn't want her to go or what this magnetic pull was he felt in his heart, but it was there, and he welcomed it. When she dropped her head and turned away from him, his heart jumped.

"I don't have time for this, Adam. Can we talk about this at home?"

"Really, Nix? You doing this now?" Adam nodded his head to the hallway that would lead them away from the group.

She bit down on her back teeth and walked off in the direction that Adam had led. She didn't want to, but she also didn't want to make a scene. The pissed off look in Airy's eyes almost made her say no, but she didn't know him like that. He couldn't be dictating what she did and didn't do. The further she walked away from him though, the more butterflies filled her stomach. It almost felt like she was making a mistake.

"I really hate him," Navi growled. "I just want her to wake the hell up already."

Airy sat quiet as he looked at the two having a quiet argument. He was pissed, but he had no right to be. Adam was *her man,* not him. She had loyalty to him, so the fact that she went to see what he wanted shouldn't have bothered him the way it did. However, he was seething on the inside, and that was always a bad thing. He had his mother's temper, and Adam was on his list. Before he did something out of character, he decided that he needed to remove himself from the situation.

"Yo, you got this, Kawan? Some shit just came up," he said, still not taking his eyes off of Nixie and Adam.

"I told yo' ass, man." Kawan shook his head and released a frustrated chuckle. "Yeah, I got it. You don't even know her. Shake that shit off, bruh." Kawan grilled his friend who laughed.

"I know enough to know that eventually she will be a part of my life. She just has to realize it and soon! I'm not built to sit around and wait, you feel me?" He gave Kawan a knowing look.

Airy wanted to lay hands on Adam for the mere fact that he had something that he wanted. No, he didn't know Nixie, but he felt her energy, and it matched his. Something he had never felt before, but he'd heard about it. His mother always told him that when he found his soul mate, he would feel her energy, and Nixie was his.

"I can't even front, I did the same shit with Navi. Something about those got damn Land women." Kawan looked down at his wife who wore a scowl. "Just wait till you meet their mama." He chuckled and received an elbow to the side. "I got this, bruh."

"Cool." Airy nodded and took off toward his office, making sure to lock eyes with Nixie before he did. He could feel her anger and hurt. The shit was weird as fuck to him, but the feeling was there. "Nigga, you gotta tighten the fuck up." He slipped his hands in his pockets and walked into his office to prepare to leave for the day the day. That whole scene just pissed him off, and work was nowhere on his agenda.

Chapter Four

LESSON 4

Sex Is Not Love

It was two in the afternoon, and Airy was sitting outside on his deck with an ice-cold Michelob Ultra in his hand. Staring out into woods that surrounded his home, his heart and mind needed a moment of peace after the way he behaved earlier that day.

If he had only felt a physical attraction to Nixie, he wouldn't even been tripping like he was, but the fact he felt an emotional force drawing them to each other took his emotions to another level completely out of his comfort zone.

Airy was never the jealousy type, but seeing Nixie leave his side to join another man annoyed him to the point where he couldn't be near her. It was crazy how one encounter could make him feel like a bitch. He chuckled at the thought. The connection wouldn't be denied.

"She got me feening for her ass, and I ain't even got the pussy yet." He lifted his beer and took a swig.

Thinking back to the first time he ever saw Nixie, he tried to remember if he felt those same sparks that he had today. He couldn't remember the butterflies and his jumping heart, but his attention was on Constance. How could he feel anything?

Sighing, he looked down at his phone and thought about all the threatening messages that he had gotten from his mother. He needed to talk to Constance and fast because he didn't see this ending very well, if or when she decided to do another pop up.

Lifting his phone to call his mother back, he was stopped when he heard his doorbell. It could have only been one of two people, and to be honest, he didn't want to see either, but one needed a talk. Pulling up his app on his phone, he looked into the camera and sighed.

"I'm not in the mood for this bullshit, but let's get it over with." He peeled himself from his chair and jogged to the door. When he opened it, he was hit with her sweet perfume instantly, and his dick jumped involuntarily. "What's up, Constance?"

Airy purposely stood in the doorway, not giving her a chance to step inside without his permission. You had to create boundaries with Constance; if you gave her an inch, she was taking twenty miles. Him standing in the door let her know that she wasn't welcomed and would only gain entry by his say so.

"Are you not going to let me in?" She pushed the door open and attempted to walk past him, but he positioned his body so that she couldn't. "Are we doing this today?"

"This is my house. You need to understand that. I'm not going back and forth with you, and I'm not doing all the dumb shit. If that's what you're on, you need to go the fuck home and now! I'm not in the mood for it."

Constance sighed and took a step back. Putting on her best pouty face, she placed her hands on his stomach and batted her eyes at him.

"That shit don't work for me anymore."

"Okay, fine. I'm here to talk. I deserve a conversation."

"You don't deserve shit but my ass to kiss after what you did. Like I said, I ain't for the bullshit today." His tall frame leaned against the door frame as he looked down into the eyes of the woman who almost broke him.

She threw her hands up in mock surrender and nodded her head. Constance had an aggressive personality, and she always got what she wanted, and Airy was what she wanted. She just couldn't give him what he wanted, and that's where their problems lied.

"I just want to talk. I love you, and I want you to hear my side of things."

"Is this gone keep you from going to my mama's house? 'Cause I can't promise the next time you go over there, she ain't gon' lay hands on you." He shrugged and opened the door so that she could walk through.

Pushing past him, she headed straight for the stairs, and he stopped her in mid stride.

"What?"

"Nah, you don't get the pleasure to experience that. You got the living room or out on the deck. Your choice." Her eyes found his as she searched them for some sort of humor or sign that he was joking but found none. "What's it gonna be?"

Smacking her lips, she stomped off toward the sliding door that led to the deck. She plopped down in the chair that was beside the one that he was sitting in. Airy could never understand how someone her age could act that way that she did.

His whole reason for getting with an older woman was the thought that he wouldn't have to deal with the childish behavior that the younger women sometimes portrayed. God played a cruel trick on him when he placed him in the path of Hurricane Constance. She was a piece of work, and she definitely taught him a lesson or two.

"How have you been, Airy? I've missed you terribly."

"I've been good, working and building. Same shit." He shrugged and took a long swig of his beer before tossing the empty bottle in the trash and reaching in the small cooler that he brought out with him and grabbing another one.

"It's a little early to be drinking, ain't it?"

"It's a little late for you to be worried about me, ain't it?"

"Airy, is this how things are gonna be with us? Like, are you going to keep walking around mad? You are not even looking at things my way. I'm forty-six years old with a son that's almost your age, and you wanted me to have another kid. I would be well past sixty at the damn kid's graduation," she fussed.

"You should have thought about that shit before you got with me. We talked about this shit; you knew I wanted kids, Constance. If you knew that was something that you didn't want, you should have told me."

"But I wanted you. Can't you see that?"

"So, you lie, then let me get you pregnant, just to kill it? And you thought that was gonna somehow be okay with me?" Airy leaned up and placed his elbows on his legs before turning to look at her.

It felt like his heart broke a second time when he observed her emotionless glare. What fucked with him the most was the fact that he didn't see one ounce of remorse in her orbs. Her whole demeanor was lax and completely lacked any kind of emotion. She really didn't care.

"I was hoping that I would be enough for you."

A deep, frustrated chuckle vibrated through his lips. There was so much that he wanted to say, but he knew that it wasn't worth it. She would never see the pain that she caused him.

"Well you weren't enough." His tone was cold and uncaring, just like her demeanor.

Constance had taken him to a dark place, one that had him wanting to put his hands on her, something that his mother taught him long ago to never do.

"How can you say that? All of the good times we had, all

of the love we made." She kneeled down in front of him and grabbed his arms, forcing him to look at her. "We were perfect for each other."

"It was all a lie."

"The way I made you feel was a lie? The way I loved you was a lie?" Her hands slowly moved up toward his thighs. "He doesn't think it was a lie." Her words were breathy and filled with lust.

Her small hands hovered over his semi hard on as she tucked her bottom lip between her teeth. A soft moan slipped her lips. When he didn't stop her, she took that as the green light to move forward. She fumbled with the button on his jeans until she had his monster free.

His backyard was completely surrounded by trees, and on the sides where it wasn't, he had a high privacy fence. They had made love under the stars many of nights, so the fact that it was broad daylight didn't bother her at all.

"This don't change shit, Constance."

She ignored what he said and hiked her short sundress over her ass. Panties weren't a necessity, because she knew exactly what she was coming over for, so she didn't bother to put any on.

When she tried to mount him, he stopped her. Leaning up enough to pull his wallet from his slacks that he still had on from earlier that day, Airy pulled the condom out and opened it up. Constance rolled her eyes and scoffed, lifting her leg so that she was standing straight up in front of him.

"Are you serious right now?"

"As a fucking heart attack." Airy never looked up. His complete focus was on him making sure that the condom was securely on his dick.

Once he was sure he was covered properly, he looked up at her. The grimace on her face was almost comical to him. He wasn't sure what she expected, but trust wasn't on the table.

"We were together for how long and have been fucking for even longer. You think I'm going to just accept the fact that you all of a sudden want to use condoms? Who is she?" She threw her hands on her well-rounded hips and glared at the man who she desperately missed being on her arm.

"There is no she."

Yet!

"You're lying. I could always tell when you were lying."

"I never lied to you, Constance, and you know it. You knew who I was when you met me. You knew what I wanted when you met me. I'm as transparent as they come." He spread his arms out wide.

"Well I don't want to feel a condom when we're making love. I want to feel you and you feel me like we always have." She seductively leaned down and grabbed the base of his dick and started to remove the condom, but Airy stopped her before she could even get started.

"Sounds like you don't want to *fuck* then." His brows knitted together while he watched the different emotional expressions contort her beautiful face. To be forty-six, Constance was attractive and in amazing shape. She didn't look a day over twenty-five.

"Airy! Why are you doing this?"

"Goodbye, Constance."

"No!" She shouted out desperately as she threw her leg across his. Lowering herself, she grabbed his dick and placed it at her opening. "I just want things to be the way they used to."

"I gave you that part of me, openly and completely; you fucked it up. You'll never get that part of me again. Ever!" He grabbed her thighs, bringing her attention to the seriousness in his tone.

Constance swallowed. Her whole plan for being there was falling apart miserably. When Airy broke up with her after he found out that she killed the baby they had made together, she knew that she had to do something. He was the kind of man that you just didn't let slip out of your hands. She knew she had to fight, and that's what she planned to do.

Airy made her feel special and wanted, something that she had been looking for her entire life. When she got pregnant, she panicked and acted irrationally. Constance only had one child, and she was okay with that until she met Airy. She thought she could finesse her way to his heart without bearing children, until she missed her period.

Now that she saw that not having kids was a deal breaker for him, she was here to try again, in hopes to bring them back together. A baby would solidify their relationship. It was something that she would just have to sacrifice. Being with Airy was worth it, and she saw that in hindsight.

"Never say never." She leaned up to kiss his lips, but he turned his head so that her lips landed on his cheek.

"Like I said, you'll *never* have that part of me again. Now you can ride this dick or move and go about your business. Your call." He shrugged.

Constance narrowed her slanted eyes at the harshness of his tone. A sensible woman would have dismounted and took her ass home, but there was no way that she could leave without showing him what he had been missing. In hopes to grant her more access to him physically and then eventually settling back into his heart.

Airy watched her nipples harden under the thin fabric of the tan sundress the minute his manhood broke her womanly barrier. The way she bit down on her bottom lip and threw her head back had his dick pulsating deep within her center. He knew he needed to control himself because this would be the last ride.

"Ummm, shit. I missed you." Constance leaned down in an attempt to kiss him again, but he moved so that his mouth connected with her exposed neck. "Ssssshhhh," she hissed.

Airy grunted in pleasure. His dick buried itself deep within her sopping core as it engulfed him in its greatness. Sex was always amazing with her. If he were honest, she was the best he had ever had thus far. However, once it was over, it was just that, over.

Grabbing her waist, he helped her find the rhythm of his pleasure, and they both settled in a lust filled bliss. Airy lifted up every time she came down on him, sending electric currents through her body. Her shoulders shook as euphoric bliss ripped through her core and spilled out on the length of him, bringing about a throaty grumble.

"Fuck, Constance."

"See, I knew you missed me." She placed her hands on his chest and began to bounce up and down on him like her life depended on it. Airy was hers, and she needed to remind him of that, so she made sure to pull out all the stops. She rolled, grinded, and bucked on his thickness, just like he liked. When he started to fuck her back from underneath, she knew she had him where she wanted him. "Yes, baby, fuck me back."

Airy wasn't about to allow her to *handle* him. That was the problem in their relationship; she thought because she was older that she could *handle* him, even in the bedroom. Planting his feet on the ground, he stood with her in his arms, never breaking their connection.

Carrying her into the house, he set her on the kitchen counter and took his massive hands and spread her legs wide as they could go. He took pleasure in watching his handiwork. Airy licked his lips and pulled out of her before slamming back in.

"Shit, Airy, baby." He pulled out again, and it was like she couldn't breathe until she felt his hardness enter her again. "Ughn, yess, just like that," she coached.

His right thumb found her love button as he slowly began to make small circles while working himself in and out of her. The tightness of her welcoming him had him in a daze, but not enough to prevent her from touching his lips, which she was continuously trying to do.

Constance knew that with Airy, kissing was the most intimate thing that you could do with a person. Lips were sacred. She never understood that, but it was the one thing that she had to *earn* with him. She needed that privilege back, but he wasn't budging.

This time when she leaned in for a kiss, he stopped and pulled out. His dick was covered in her juices and throbbing to be back inside her, but not at the expense of his heart.

"Turn around." His chest heaved up and down while he looked down at her short frame.

"Why, I just wanted to—"

"Turn the fuck around." His authoritative tone sent chills down her spine, around to her pussy, causing it to pulsate. She loved when he got aggressive in the bedroom.

Turning around, Constance tooted her ass up, just the way he liked it. Airy grabbed one of her legs and threw it on top of the counter and slid back in. Grabbing her waist, he watched as his dick disappeared and then appeared again. Licking his lips, he grabbed her shoulders and pushed her down onto the counter to improve the arch in her back.

"Just like that."

His strokes sped up, and throughout the house, all you could hear was skin slapping and Constance moaning. Glancing at him over her shoulder made her bite down on her lip. The sweat that covered his brows and upper lip was sexy to her. What she would do to kiss his lips again. She wasn't going to push her luck. *For now!*

"Airy, I'm about to cum, baby. Shit, that feels so good. God, I've missed thisssssss." She moaned out, sending her eyes to the back of her head and an indescribable moan to escape her lips. "Ohhhhh my God!" She screamed as she released all over Airy, followed by slight shaking of her legs.

Airy had to grab her by the waist to hold her in place for a few more strokes until he quickly pulled out and jacked himself until he filled up the condom. He stumbled backwards and had to catch himself with the island that sat in the middle of the kitchen floor.

"Fuck!"

Regret filled him instantly as he thought about what he had just done. He had been semi successful at creating somewhat of a boundary when it came to Constance, and all of that just went out the window, all because his hormones and emotions were all over the place from his run in with the beautiful Nixie.

What the fuck did I just do?

"See, I knew you missed me like I missed you. There was no way that you could handle my body like that and hadn't been thinking about it. You tore my ass up, and I loved every minute." Constance leaned against the counter with her pointer finger planted between her teeth in a sexual manner.

"We fucked. It was good, but that's all it was. Don't think too much into it."

"That's what your mouth say, but your actions said something totally different." She giggled as she took a few seductive steps in his direction. "I mean, look at him, still standing for me." She reached for his dick, but he slapped her hands away. "Baby, you still love me, and you know it; but if you want to keep playing this game, I'll play with you." Constance rolled her eyes.

"That's where you're wrong, Cee," he said, calling her by the nickname that he gave her while they were dating. "Sex isn't love. My dick did the same thing with you as it did with the bitch I fucked last night."

Constance threw her hand over her mouth and stared at him with a shocked expression. She couldn't believe his revelation about sleeping with another woman.

"How dare you?"

"I'm single as fuck!" Airy yelled, towering over her. "I'm not sure what you thought you were getting coming over, but a hard dick was all I had to offer. Guest bathroom is right there. Clean up and bounce."

She looked at him, and again, there was no sign of humor in sight. Shaking her head, Constance stomped off to the guest bathroom while Airy jogged up the stairs to his. He made sure that the condom was still intact before rolling it off and tossing it in the trash.

Silently cursing himself, he grabbed a washcloth and began to clean himself off. He knew that he couldn't leave her in his house too long, so a shower was out of the question. Once he handled his hygiene, he pulled his vibrating phone out of his slacks that he had just secured on his waist.

"Sup, Ma?"

"I ought to drive over there and beat your ass," Anna fussed. She didn't know what had gotten into her only son, but she was determined to get to the bottom of it.

"What's up with all the violence? You didn't have a good time on your trip?" He smiled to himself.

"This is not a joke. You hung up on me earlier after cursing at me and then talking about some daughter-in-law. It better not be that old bitch."

Airy placed his fist over his mouth to attempt to cover his laugh, but it was no use. He burst out laughing.

Anna never liked Constance, and she never missed a second to let him know how she felt. They were too close in age for that woman to be dating her son. When they broke up, Anna thought she would shout all over her house.

"I didn't curse at you, Ma. This woman walked into my office while I was on the phone with you, and I swear I fell in love the minute her cheeks met her eyes." Airy smiled to himself, thinking about Nixie.

"Airy, you said the same thing about the old bitch."

"Ma, stop calling her old! You're older than she is." Airy chuckled.

"Not by much, and that's the issue. Baby, you're still young. I want grandbabies. Her old seasoned ass eggs are in the same reject line as mine," Anna said with a scoff.

"That's fucked up for you to even say, Ma." Airy shook his head as if she could see him. "But the girl that came into my office was... I don't know how to describe her. Remember when you told me that I would know when I've found my soulmate because I would feel their energy?"

"Yes, I do remember that, but I think you be imagining things, baby."

"I'll holla at you later, Ma." Airy hung up the phone and shook his head. He knew that she would be calling back or popping up at some point, but right now, he needed to get Constance out of his house and do some soul searching.

.

Chapter Five

LESSON 5

Love Is Give And Take

"I can't believe how dope that fucking building was." Nixie beamed as Navi pulled up to her house and turned the car off. "It was like it was fucking perfect. I'm super excited."

"Airy said he knew what you liked. You just better hope you didn't piss him off and he put it on the market." Navi chuckled to herself.

Nixie glared at her sister before slamming herself back in the seat. She hated that Airy didn't come with them to see the building that he picked out. It was something about the chocolate god that she couldn't quite shake. He had been plaguing her thoughts since the look he gave her before he walked into his office and slammed the door.

"His sexy ass," she groaned. "Ugh! This sucks, but I got too much going on anyway to pull anyone into my bullshit, Navi. It's best I keep my distance." Nixie pouted.

Navi rolled her eyes and released a frustrated chuckle. "I wish you wake the fuck up, sister. That man don't give a fuck about you. He works for a realty company, and until now, he didn't even think about helping set you up with anything. And I don't know if you noticed, but after he saw that Airy was out of the way, so was his desire to make sure you had what you needed." Navi cut her eyes at her sister.

She was right. Before Airy walked in his office and slammed his door, Adam was telling Nixie that he would help her get a building, but the minute he was out of sight, so was his plan to help. Adam was selfish, and it was extremely unattractive.

"I knew that he couldn't help me from the beginning. He works in the finance department. What could he do for me when I don't need financing?" Nixie said matter-of-factly. "I know what he was doing. Trust me, Navi, I'm not as naive as you think I am."

"I don't think you're naïve. I think you believe in second chances, even when people don't deserve them." Navi sighed. "At least shoot Airy a text apologizing for what happened today." A sneaky smirk appeared on her face as she dug around her pocketbook and handed her a card.

"You little sneaky bitch." Nixie giggled. "When the hell did you snatch this up?"

"Don't worry about what I do. Just know that I got you, even when you don't got yourself." She winked and nodded her head. "Now get the fuck out. I promised my husband all kind of shit for trying to play matchmaker for your ass to fuck it up anyway. Now my got damn jaws gon' be sunken." She sucked her jaws in like she was a fish.

Nixie burst out laughing. "Yo, something is seriously wrong with you, Navi. I swear mama smoked weed or something. What the fuck!" Nixie folded over, holding her stomach.

"I'm serious. He was pissed at me for trying to get him to go home and then changing my mind. Then your ass." Navi playfully rolled her eyes. "So yeah, I'm sure he's already home waiting."

"Well go do what you gotta do, baby. I'll see you tomorrow."

"Send Airy a text, hoe. If to only make sure that he ain't gon' put the building on the market before you get a chance to snatch it up." Navi gave her a knowing look, causing Nixie to shake her head. "I'm serious, Nix. You deserve better, and who knows. Mr. Chocolate God might just be your better. You didn't see how pissed he got at you?"

Navi told her how mad Airy got when she decided to walk off with Adam. She also disclosed that he put claims on her with a time clock attached. Nixie didn't know how she felt about that, but it did feel good to have someone checking for her the way he was.

"I will." Nixie shut the door in hopes that the conversation was over. When Navi rolled down her window, she knew that she didn't have such luck.

"I'm not playing with you. Don't make me take matters into my own hands. You know I will."

Nixie cringed as she thought about her sister taking charge in this situation. Shaking her head, she glared at her as if she were daring her to do so. When Navi laughed and rolled up the window, Nixie flipped her off until she was fully out of the driveway.

Laughing, she made her way into the house, kicked off the peep toe pumps she wore, and threw herself on the sofa. Her eyes went to the card that she had in her hands as she twirled it around between her middle and pointer finger.

Groaning as thoughts of Airy from earlier rushed back to her mind sending her heart into a frenzy, right before guilt attacked the butterflies that had swarmed her belly. She should not have been lusting over another man when she still had baggage at home.

"Grounds for disaster." She shook her head and laughed. "But I do owe him an apology."

No, bitch. You just want to spark up a conversation with his tall, chocolate ass. Don't even try it.

Sighing, she gave into the strong urge to just hear his voice again. She knew it was wrong, and she knew that it would more than likely cause more problems than she was prepared to deal with. However, something was pulling her to dial those ten numbers, and she wasn't inclined to disappoint.

Taking in a sharp breath, she placed the phone to her ear as she waited for his profound declaration to seep through the sound waves of the phone. She hadn't realized she was holding her breath until she heard the voicemail click on, as she hurried to hang up before it caught her breathing.

"That's what you get for trying to be a whore." She scolded herself with a soft chuckle. Shaking her head, she stood from the sofa as she headed to the kitchen, but before she could turn the corner, her phone sounded.

For a second, she just stood there debating on whether or not she would answer it or let it ring. Hell, she didn't even know if it was him, but she was anxious to find out.

Thirsty bitch.

She chuckled at the thought as she made a dash for her phone before it stopped ringing. Once it was in her hand, she stared at the number before sliding the green answer button over.

"Airy Menz."

Nixie had to force herself not to let out the blissful moan that crept up in her throat at the sound of his voice. Her pussy pulsated, something that it hadn't done in quite some time. At that point, she knew just how much of a mistake it was to call him.

But I just want to apologize, right?

"Hello... Airy Menz speaking."

"He-hey um hi-hello." Nixie stammered, instantly slapping herself in the forehead for sounding so... juvenile.

"Ms. Land, nice to hear from you." A smooth yet throaty chuckle floated through the phone. He was excited that he wasn't the only one with thoughts of the other. "I heard you really liked the building."

"O.M.G. I freaking loved it. Everything about it screamed Nix Beauty, and I can't wait for the keys to be in my hand."

Her enthusiasm had Airy on the other end of the phone smiling like he had just hit the lottery.

"I told you, I knew exactly what you liked."

The line went silent for a second. Nixie had to stop herself from saying something slick back. She didn't want to throw out mixed signals, so she took a few seconds to gather her thoughts before she spoke again.

"You sure are good at what you do. Within minutes of meeting me and barely any conversation, you got it on the first try."

"It was the connection," Airy said boldly.

"Ex-excuse me?" Nixie heard him loud and clear, but she wanted to hear him say it again. She felt a connection to him too, but she made herself believe that it was just physical.

"Is your *man* home?"

"No, but—" she started, but the line going dead stopped her. She looked at the phone and furrowed her brows in. "This negro hung up the damn..." Her words trailed off. She watched a number she didn't know go across her screen, signaling that she had a FaceTime call. "What the—"

"I need to see your beautiful face, but I didn't want to cause you any more problems."

Nixie fought the smile that was tugging against her lips, but she failed miserably. Sweat hovered along her brow as her cheeks flushed a soft shade of pink.

"Ahhh, she blushes." Airy's perfectly white teeth spread across the screen, causing Nixie to roll her eyes. "Airy one... said obstacle by the name of Adam zero."

The mention of Adam's name put a sour taste in Nixie's mouth. The way he behaved today was something that she had never seen before, and she couldn't wait to lay eyes on him so she could tell him that she didn't appreciate it. It also reminded her that her reason for calling Airy wasn't to grin all in his face but indeed thank him and apologize for her *boyfriend's* actions.

"About that—"

"If you're about to apologize for him, stop it. You didn't do anything wrong. You are not responsible for his actions or his *insecurities*."

Airy's smile disappeared. His passion filled stare was paired with a set of knitted bushy brows showcasing his aggravation with the thought of her apologizing for Adam's idiocrasy.

"I know, but still. I never meant to bring that to your place of business. Had I been upfront with him and not on my petty shit, he would have been aware and not so... accusing." She shook her head while rolling her eyes.

"As long as the end game was me getting to meet you, it was all worth it in my book." Lust dripped from his tone, and the eagerness to know about Nixie danced around his orbs. She could feel a closeness to him, even though he was nowhere near.

"Thank you." Her eyes cast down, away from the camera. His intense stare was causing things to stir up in her that she hadn't felt since she met Adam. Things that one needed to feel, loved and wanted. Things she shouldn't be feeling from another man. "Well I won't hold you. I just wanted to apo—thank you for *knowing* what I was looking for and making me a happy woman today." She smiled as she gave him her attention again.

"If you give me the chance, I'll make you happy every day."

"Airy, I—"

"Let's talk about it another time." He winked into the camera right as Nixie heard keys jingling in the door. "I'll let you go, beautiful. Have an amazing rest of your day, and I can't wait to see you again. Lock my number in. I'm here if you need anything."

Nixie opened her mouth to say something, but he was gone before she could. She should have been grateful, because a scowl wearing Adam walked through the door just seconds later, but in reality, she felt a little sad, almost empty.

Laying her phone in her lap, she closed her eyes, trying to get herself together, but the more she tried, the more she thought about Airy.

Get it together, Nix. You don't even know this man!

Sighing, her fingers made their way to her temples as she slowly started to massage them. She hadn't even acknowledged Adam, and he was pissed about it. Her mind was on Airy. Even though she didn't know him, he was sexily intriguing, so much so, he was slowly taking over her entire thought process.

"So, are we going to talk about this?" Adam slipped his

hands in his pockets as he looked down at the back of Nixie's head. "I mean, you act like what you did today was okay."

"And exactly what did I do, Adam?" Nixie sat back on the couch, still not bothering to look at him. She knew that this conversation was coming, but she had to admit that she wasn't prepared for it.

"You embarrassed me!"

"How so, Adam?" Her nonchalant attitude was fueling an already blazing fire within him, and he was close to blowing up.

"You came to my job, didn't even fucking tell me, and then you act like a common whore!"

The way Nixie's head snapped around had him regretting the words he'd spoke. He was just mad that Airy had his eyes on his woman. Deep down, he knew that what he was feeling at the moment didn't really have anything to do with Nixie but more so of his own insecurities, but he couldn't help but lash out. As his woman, she was supposed to protect his fears, and she wasn't.

"I'm going to pretend like you didn't say that, and I'm going to go to my sister's house." She stood and grabbed her phone and keys from the coffee table next to the couch. "You real close to snatching up yo' single tag because if you ever in your got damn life call me out my name again, you won't have to worry about who I'm being a whore for, because you won't be here to witness it." Her brows hitched as she offered up a slight nod in his direction.

"No, we need to talk about this. I'm sorry for saying you

were acting like a whore, but you have to see where I was coming from," he pleaded. "I work for real estate; you could have come to me."

"How many times did I tell you that I was thinking about opening up a storefront?" Her hands went to her shapely hips. "How many times have you heard me complain about my kitchen being too small to handle all the orders that I was doing? Huh? How many fucking times?"

"But you never asked me to help you."

"How fucking dumb are you, Adam? I shouldn't have had to ask, because you should've known! When you need me to pick you up a suit because you have a gala or an event to go to, do you have to ask me?" She tilted her head.

"No, but—"

"Nah, you don't get to *but* this out. You don't *have* to tell me because I care enough about you. I pay enough attention to what the fuck you need to know what I need to do to make your life easier! I don't get the same in return! And frankly, I'm sick of this one-sided ass relationship." Nixie shook her head. "Love is supposed to be give and take, but I ain't getting shit out this!" She rolled her eyes and headed for the door.

"How is this relationship one-sided?"

"Because I'm expected to be what you need, be there when you need me, and to be who you want me to be, while you get to bitch and complain about nothing, and I'm sick of it. I'm giving you the same energy you give me from now on. It's time to focus on me and what I *need*."

"What kind of woman says that when they're in a relationship!" Adam yelled to her departing back.

The fresh air hit Nixie, urging her to take in a deep breath. What she didn't want was the tears that followed her exhale. Shaking her head, she roughly wiped the few that managed to escape. She was tired of feeling alone and not important. The worse part was she didn't see it getting any better.

Chapter Six

LESSON 6

Love Requires Attention

"Ayeeee!" Nixie and Navi yelled at the same time. "Heard It All Before" by Sunshine Anderson blared through the speakers at The Roxbury. They both rushed the dance floor with drinks in hand.

When Nixie arrived at her sister's house, pissed off about the argument that she and Adam had, Navi suggested they come out and have a good time. She was sick of her sister having to deal with all the bullshit and thought she needed a night out, and she was right. They were having a great time.

"Come home late, seems you barely beat the sun," they sang off key.

Nixie didn't drink heavy; she loved a glass or two of wine, but she shied away from hard liquor, although tonight, she needed it. After three Jäger Bombs, she was pumped and

ready to party. The Jäger paired with the Red Bull was enough
to have her carefree and having the time of her life.

"I heard it all before!" Nixie yelled over the music as she
wound her hips to the beat.

Navi knew then that her sister was lit. She thought it was
funny but knew that those three shots were probably her
limit. Water was going to be her drink of choice for the rest
of the night.

"Damn, nigga, you gon' blink?" Kawan released a low,
teasing chuckle.

Airy hadn't taken his eyes off of Nixie the entire night. He
was excited that he decided to take Kawan up on his offer to
step out, because if he hadn't, he would have missed a chance
to spend time with and get to know Nixie.

Lust oozed from Airy's pores. It was no secret that he
wanted Nixie, and he wasn't trying to hide it. She still wore
the black linen pants from earlier, and her belly button was
still exposed, displaying the sexy chain around it. He was
intrigued and dying to know more about the beautiful woman
who had owned his thoughts for the whole day.

"If I blink, I might miss something." Airy glanced at
Kawan and then turned his attention back to Nixie who was
staring right back at him. The way she was rolling her hips
while smirking at him had his dick rock hard, and he didn't
want anyone but her to relieve it.

He slowly moved his hand down and adjusted his hard on
to attempt to relieve some of the pressure. Nixie's attention

went to what he was doing. Her tongue dragged across her bottom lip, bringing a smirk to Airy's face.

"Aye, cut that bullshit out!" Kawan yelled over the music before shooting an evil glare at Nixie, who laughed and hugged on her sister as the two continued to dance around the club.

"Shorty is fucking with my mental," Airy said more to himself than to Kawan.

"I told your ass not to do this, but nah, you don't want to listen. I'm telling you now, if y'all shit makes its way into my home, I'm getting at both of you." Kawan pointed back and forth between Nixie and Airy. "This is a fucked-up situation because you my boy, but I've chilled with her boyfriend. I don't care for his uppity ass, but I've broke bread with him."

"What you trying to say, nigga?" Airy's cocky smirk slowly slid onto his face.

"I ain't trying to say shit. I'm telling you that this is fucked up on all ends. Sis needs to end whatever the fuck she got going on with him before y'all even think about it."

Kawan hated the feeling that fell over him. He didn't want to be in the middle of mess, but when it came down to it, his loyalty was to Airy, and he knew it.

"I feel you, but sometimes you can't ignore that gut feeling, and my gut is telling me that she," he nodded in Nixie's direction, "is someone that I'm supposed to have in my life, and I ain't talking about no got damn friendship either."

"I'm sure her nigga would have an issue with that."

"Giving a fuck has never been my strong suit." A chuckle laced in sarcasm slipped from his lips.

What he said was true. He didn't give a damn about Nixie's boyfriend one way or another. As far as he was concerned, he was just a placeholder until their stars aligned, which would be sooner rather than later.

"I hear you." Kawan grabbed his beer and took down the rest of it as he pushed himself off of the bar. There was no need in trying to convince him to keep his distance. His eyes were on Nixie, and the determination that rested in them let Kawan know that he was wasting his time. "I'm going to dance with my wife."

"That's a good ass idea." Kawan looked at Airy and shook his head, bringing them both into a fit of laughter. "You may as well get used to it, nigga. I'm about to be brother-in-law." The confidence in his words was just as powerful as what came out of his mouth. Airy was going to have Nixie, and that was all there was to it.

The two men made it on the dance floor right as the deejay switched the song to something a little slower. "Promise" by Jagged Edge blared through the speakers. Airy grabbed Nixie by the hand and pulled her to him, allowing his hands to rest on the small of her back. Her hands snaked around his neck, and their eyes connected.

"Kismet," Airy leaned down and whispered in her ear. When her brows knitted and she cocked her head to the side, he chuckled at her confused expression. "It means fate in Turkish. Do you believe in fate, Nixie?"

She thought about what he asked her. Did she believe in fate? She thought that her and Adam meeting was fate, and you see how that turned out for her. Nixie took in a deep breath to deliver her conclusion, but she was stopped by the intense smell of his cologne that took over her sense of smell momentarily. The subtle woodsy, wrapped in the softness of bergamot with a sweet musk on the back end was enough to send a trail of shivers down her back across her waist and straight to her...

Nixie cleared her throat of her nasty thoughts. "No!"

"No what?" Airy had gotten so lost in the feel of her in his arms that the conversation that he started was the last thing on his mind.

"No, I don't believe in fate. I believe that everything happens for a reason though."

Airy nodded. "Well we're going to have to change that, beautiful. Yes, everything happens for a reason, but sometimes, it's fate. Things are supposed to happen; things are supposed to move around because that's how it was designed. All part of God's plan." Leaning down, he placed a soft kiss on her cheek.

"So how do you explain the fuck ups that look like fate in the beginning?" Their eyes connected as he waited for her to elaborate, which she never did.

"Fate is not only good. Sometimes things need to happen to teach us lessons, especially when it comes to love. People are meant to come into your life for a season so they can teach you, prepare you for your forever." Airy secured his hands around her waist as they continued to sway while Jagged Edge finished up their crooning session. "Just like with your skin care products. You had to *learn* to do it to become good at it. You didn't just wake up one day and mixed the perfect batch and say, yep, I'm a pro."

"And who says I didn't?" Nixie placed her hands on her hips and looked up at him with her head cocked to the side, something that Airy noticed she did when she was challenging you.

Airy removed her hands from her hips and moved her back into his space. He shook his head and kissed her forehead. The thick lips against her skin had her kitty purring and dying to be petted, but she refrained from offering up an advance. She wanted to hear more about these *lessons*.

"What I'm trying to say is, it took you a few times to get it right, and once you did, you had a masterpiece." He stopped once the song ended and looked down at her, waiting to see if what he said registered with her. "Sometimes it takes a few fuck ups to finally get it right, and when you get it right, you hold on to it and don't accidentally include the fuck ups."

Her loaded gaze fell on his. There were so many things going through her mind at that present moment. Everything he said was the truth. Adam was her second failed relationship, but in her heart, she knew that love was out there for her. Whether it was in Airy or not, she didn't know, but she damn sure wouldn't mind finding out.

Nixie, you gotta a whole man at home!

Sighing, she dropped her head, and Airy used his pointer

finger to force her eyes on his. Uncertainty swirled around her eyes, and he hated that. He wanted her to be sure about everything, including her being there with him, but he knew her situation. She needed time to figure out what she wanted and what she needed. He would give her that, as long as she continued to get to know him. That wasn't fair, but neither was love.

"I—I—" she started, but his lips meeting hers silenced her.

For a second, Nixie stood there, stunned. The ever so bold Airy took his moment, and she wasn't upset about it. After a moment, she kissed him back, with logical thought slipping away. Nothing else mattered to her in this moment but the connection that she felt from the touch of his thick lips.

Taking the kiss deeper, Nixie was suddenly overwhelmed by emotions that started and stopped with Airy. The way his lips felt amazing against hers, had her dreaming about how they would feel in other places. His hands traveled lower and cupped her ass, making her pussy jump. The way he grunted made her feel as if he felt it, but he couldn't, *could he?*

Adam had never in the history of their relationship kissed her like this and—*Adam!* Nixie pulled away from Airy, and her hands went straight to her mouth. She looked up into Airy's eyes. She was on fire for him, and it was wrong. Even though Adam was a dick, her loyalty was still to him, for now.

"I'm sorry." She turned to run off, but Airy was on her heels. The minute the night air hit her, she stumbled back a little and fell right into the arms of Airy. "I'm sorry, Airy. I didn't mean to make you think—"

"You didn't make me think anything. I did what I did because I wanted to. Because in my heart, I felt that shit, and I don't disobey my heart." He smirked. His whole aura was contagious, so it wasn't surprising that a smile made its way onto her face. "But I am sorry for not thinking of you and how you felt about it. My heart can be selfish at times when it comes to something it wants."

Her cheeks warmed up, and her hands became sweaty. She could have sworn that she could hear the ticks of her heartbeat. Reason and logic were tipping again, and it was becoming hard to not give into his sexiness, but she couldn't do that. That wasn't her, but this man was making it so hard.

"As bad as I want to fold and give in to everything I know you can give, the reality of it is I got a situation."

"A situation that doesn't make you happy."

"True, but a situation, nonetheless," Nixie said and pushed her sweaty curls out of her face. She knew that she would feel all of the dancing that she was doing tomorrow, but she couldn't say it wasn't worth it.

"You're right." It was like her breathing stopped for a second. He was giving her what she wanted, but the thought of not seeing him again brought a weird feeling in her chest. "I'll back off, but I'm not going away." She released the breath she didn't know she was holding. "I feel this insanely strong connection, and I know you feel that shit too. I can see it in your eyes." His hands cupped the side of her face as he brought her to him and kissed her forehead. "But I get it, and I won't disrespect your *situation* if you promise me one thing."

"What's that?" She was almost afraid to ask, but her curiosity got the best of her.

"That we get to know each other." He took a step closer to her. "As friends, for now. That way, when he messes up, and he will because he doesn't know what kind of woman he has on his arm, I'll done already put the work in."

"Airy, that's not fair."

"Love's not fair, but we all yearn for it." Leaning down, he placed a soft kiss on her lips.

Desire gathered and solidified in her being, but she practiced self-control. As bad as she wanted to go in for another kiss, she refrained. Clearing her throat, she took a small step backwards to create a little space, causing Airy to chuckle.

"This is gonna be hard," Nixie whined.

"If it was easy, it wouldn't be worth it." He winked and grabbed her hand. "Come on. Let's go enjoy the rest of the night. I promise to keep my lips to myself." He chuckled.

"For some reason, I don't even believe you." She groaned but never removed herself from his hold.

Chapter Seven

LESSON 7

Love Is Learned

"How have my girls been?" Natalia walked down the small hill, onto the deck, and then lowered herself to the edge of the pool.

She glanced over to Navi, who was to her left, and then turned her attention to her baby girl, who was floating around the pool with a strapless, leopard print one piece that had the entire left side cut out.

"*I've* been good." Navi smirked while Nixie threw daggers her way. "Your baby, on the other hand, has a horrible case of the bitch ass boyfriend blues that she can't seem to shake."

Since the fight Nixie had with Adam, things had gone even further downhill. If he wasn't accusing her of sleeping with Airy behind his back, then he was complaining about her spending so much time working on opening her shop. Nixie couldn't win with him, and she was tired of trying.

On the other hand, Airy had been the best distraction. They talked and FaceTimed every day. He'd even made it his business to be as involved with her transition to her shop, as she allowed.

"What's going on, baby?" Natalia's worried glare met Nixie.

Natalia always worried that Nixie would be more like her than she would have liked. She had a huge heart and forgave too often and too easy, accepting things that she didn't necessarily have to, with the thought of people possibly *getting it right*. That had been Natalia so many years ago, and although she didn't regret it, if she could go back and change it, she would.

"Same old shit with Adam."

"He's jealous of her, and instead of getting on top of his game, he's trying to knock her off hers." Navi shrugged as they both looked at her. "What? She was going to give you the watered-down version." She shrugged, and Natalia shook her head.

Navi was her firecracker. She didn't care what she said and who she said it to, and if she hurt your feelings, that was your problem. She loved that about her daughter, but sometimes her outspokenness drove her crazy.

"I confronted him about not showing up to the pop-up shop. He said that he had a job and didn't have time to be my *cheerleader*. Pretty much said that he didn't believe in me and wasn't going to kiss my ass because of my accomplishments. At least that's what I got out of it." Nixie picked up the mixed drink that was in the cup holder of her float and took a sip. "Adam is a selfish asshole, and he wants to be an alpha male, and he thinks because I don't follow after his every word that I'm not allowing him to be that."

"I agree with Navi. Adam has some deep-rooted mommy issues. He doesn't want you to succeed out of fear that you won't need him anymore. The fact that you are pushing through creates a jealous barrier, which prevents him from loving you the way you deserve to be loved," Natalia said. "Listen, baby. If a man loves you, he's going to support whatever journey you choose to embark on, even if he doesn't agree. He won't try and stifle your drive or commitment."

"I know, Mommy," Nixie said, leaning her head back to prevent the tears that were begging to fall. "It's just... I just... ugh... I don't know."

She was right about one thing; Adam did have mommy issues. That should have been a red flag for Nixie when he told her about his mother, but instead, she thought that she could help him heal. Now it was blowing up in her face.

Adam's mother left him and his father when he was a teenager. She was a writer for the local tribune, and she was amazing at it. A nationally known magazine caught hold of one of her stories and convinced her to start freelance writing for them and a few of their counterparts, offering her money that she couldn't turn down.

Senior, Adams dad, didn't want her to do it. He told her that a wife's job was home, taking care of her husband and kids, giving her an ultimatum, if she took the job, he was going to divorce her, and she could never see Adam again. Adam's mom loved her son, but she couldn't live like a prisoner anymore, so she left and embedded a host of issues within Senior and Adam.

"When you told me about that, I wanted to tell you to run away, far away, but by that time, you were already smitten with him. I was hoping that my intuition was wrong, but it looks like it wasn't."

"Nope, it wasn't, and I'm just waiting on her to drop his ass." Navi interjected with a smirk on her face.

"It's not that simple. I've been with this man for three years, and I can't sit here and lie and say that it's been all bad. We've had good times." Nixie tried to make some sense of her situation, but the more she listened and talked out loud, the more she was starting to realize that she had been holding on to a... *hope*. "I just thought that he would realize what he was doing and get better. I care about him, and I have love for him. I guess I just... I don't know what I thought."

"You thought that your love for him would change him, and that can't happen. The way you love is learned; your upbringing, your environment, it all gives us our love language. If you are brought up to think that women are only supposed to cater to home and it's betrayal if they don't, that way of thinking is learned, that *love* is learned. Do you understand what I'm saying?"

"But he started out so sweet and loving. I don't remember when there was a time that he didn't think about me." Sighing heavily, Nixie groaned.

"And when did all that change, baby?"

"When she quit working for Duke and started working for her damn self. He don't want an independent boss bitch. He wants a broke bitch that will need and cater to his needs. If you ask me, he ain't a real man at all. Now Airy... that's a man." Navi stuck her tongue out but immediately straightened her face when she caught the evil glare from her husband.

"Who is Airy?"

"No one, Mommy." Nixie snapped at her sister who wore a skittish smile. Shaking her head, Nixie turned her attention to her mother. "I just don't know what to do. He thinks that I'm sleeping with my realtor, which I am *not!*" That comment was definitely directed at her sister who offered up a smirk. "He also feels like I put my business before him and our relationship."

"That's an excuse for him to act an ass, and you know it." Navi shook her head as she stood up and headed to their outside bar to fix her another drink. "And I couldn't tell when he had his tongue down your throat." She stuck her tongue out at Nixie, who covered her face in embarrassment.

"Navi!" Natalia chastised her oldest daughter. She giggled and continued on to the bar to grab her a drink. "Where did I go wrong with her?" She looked up to the sky as if she was praying. "Ummmhmmm, we'll talk about that later." Natalia glared at her youngest baby whose face was beet red. "Tell me though, how do you feel?"

"I feel like this relationship has ran its course. I honestly don't think we should have been together this long, but I always thought that maybe I could turn it around. Now, I see that I can't. Adam and I want two different things in life."

"Well, baby, don't make that man feel like there is a possibility for a future when you know it's not. Let him go, and you move on, if that's how you feel." Natalia's soft tone was comforting and nonjudgmental. It gave Nixie the confidence that she needed. "And one more thing." She cringed when her mother smirked before one of her brows hitched. "Whoever this *Airy* is, make sure you are completely done with Adam before you involve someone else in your mess. It's grounds for disaster."

"I won't. I respect him too much to do that. He's my realtor and Kawan's colleague. We don't even know each other really. We've met once, but I do talk to him on the phone." The thought of him sent a swarm of butterflies into her stomach, and she couldn't stop the smile that perched its way onto her sun kissed face.

"You don't know him, but you like him?"

"It's more of a scary yet exhilarating connection that has me sexily intrigued."

"In layman's terms, she wants to fuck his brains out."

"Navi Lanae Land Marks! Watch your damn mouth."

"Sorry, Mommy. That one slipped." She giggled as she took her seat next to her mother. "But she does. Look at her." She nodded to her sister who was shaking her head.

"I do not want—"

"Yes, you do," Natalia said, cutting her off. "I can tell by the way your cheeks turn bright red at his name. Don't open up one door before you completely close the next. If two doors are opened at the same time, they are bound to bang against one another at some point." She raised her brows.

"I know." Her eyes cast down like she was a child being punished for her wrongdoings.

"But... I don't want you to be like me and stay in a relationship for anything other than love." Natalia looked at both of her daughters. "I took a lot of shit from your father, all because I wanted the best for you. I didn't work and didn't have anything to show for myself or you guys, and he made sure of it. I knew he was cheating, and I knew that he had built a life with the other woman. None of that mattered because I had fell out of love a long time ago. My sole purpose was to make sure that y'all had what you needed."

"Mom..." Navi said, turning to face her mother.

They had never heard her talk about life with their father or why she decided to stay with him after everything that he put her through. It was one of the main reasons that Navi's heart was so hard, and she didn't take shit from people, just like it was the reason that Nixie loved to give people chances.

"What are you saying?" Nixie had dismounted her float and made her way to the two women she looked up to the most.

"I'm saying that I knew everything that your father was doing. I allowed him to treat me like I was nothing to him so that I could make sure that you two," she pointed at the both of them, "would never have to go through the same thing.

Navi, when you turned eighteen is when things really started to get bad, but he was up for city councilman. A divorce would have killed his chances for election, so I told him that if he put you through school that I would stay with him." She smiled. "He didn't want to; he was like Adam and his father. He didn't think that women should be educated, but I didn't want that for my girls, so I stayed."

"I don't know what to say." Navi wiped a stray tear from her face. A part of her always looked at her mother as weak for taking all that she did, but to know that she did it for her wellbeing made her see her in a new light.

"Don't you dare cry. That's what you do when you're a mother, and if your stubborn ass would give me a grandbaby, then you'll know what I mean." She smirked and then nodded to Kawan who slowly started clapping.

"This is not about me right now." Navi waved them off, drawing a scoff from Kawan, followed by a few mumbles.

"But he ended up leaving anyway." Nixie's brows furrowed questioningly.

"Yes. Once it was your turn to graduate, my dear, he was in the middle of a term and figured that he didn't need me. That he had time to twist some things around in his favor, but he didn't know that I kept receipts. So in order for the divorce to go his way, then he was to put you through school. I got my way, and he got his."

"You didn't have to do that. You lost everything." Nixie wanted to see where her head was at.

"No the hell I didn't." She frowned at Nixie. "I gained

everything! You both got educated from Ivy league schools. I regained my independence and sanity. I won."

"But he left you with nothing." That was Navi.

"He offered a very hefty alimony settlement, but taking his money would keep me connected to him, and I didn't want it. I wanted to be done, so that's what I did." Natalia smiled. "I made him do the one thing he hated and that was give me the money to go back to school, which I did and made an amazing living for *myself*. It was the best feeling in the world. I knew that I couldn't do that while raising you and making sure that you both got what you needed to succeed. So I sacrificed for what I loved."

"Oh my God, Mommy. We didn't know."

"I didn't mean for you to know. I did what I had to do for y'all, and if that meant putting up with an incompetent, inconsiderate, impotent—"

"Whoa!" They both yelled simultaneously.

Natalia laughed and pushed her curly locks out of her face. "I'm just saying. I did what I had to do so that you two would never have to, and I need you to know that. Maybe I went about it the wrong way, but I did the only thing I knew how."

"All this time, I looked at you staying as being weak. I promised myself that I would never be like that. It's the only reason that I don't do second chances. It's the reason I'm so cold and closed off at times," Navi said. "It's also the only reason that I'm so hard on Nixie because I didn't want her to *be like you*."

"I got your nerve." Natalia grilled her daughter before she

broke out into the biggest smile. "I learned about love through my parents, your grandparents, God rest their souls. They were the epitome of black love, and I knew after the first five years that I was with your father that it wasn't love. However, the minute I laid eyes on Stan, I knew he was my forever."

"Aww." The girls crooned, causing Natalia to swat at them both.

"I just want you to be happy. I did what I did so that you could have a real chance at love. Now I see that my methods may have tainted your way a little. I'm sorry about that, but the goal was still the same. I wanted you to be independent and love with your whole hearts. Nixie, if Adam ain't for you, let him go. Don't wait around for the worst; your heart knows." She nodded.

"Stan, my man!" Kawan yelled out and walked over to greet his father-in-law. "Thank God. I was tired of all this estrogen." He glanced over and smirked at the evil glares he received.

"You on your own, son." Stan chuckled. "I sleep beside the mama bear."

Everyone burst out laughing as they continued to enjoy their day. Nixie's mind was flooded with everything that her and her mother had talked about. She knew that she needed to make a decision, but was she prepared for it?

Chapter Eight

LESSON 8

Love Is Focusing On Quality, Not Quantity.

"Ah! I can't believe this is mine!" Nixie squealed and jumped up and down as she watched the graphic designer put the finishing touches on her window décor. Her logo was perfect and more than she could ever ask for.

Looking down at her, he couldn't help the smile that graced his face. It matched the one that she wore perfectly. For a while, nothing was said. Both barely breathing, they just dwelled in the moment, lost in the essence of their attraction. It felt real and right, but Nixie knew that she still had baggage, so she was the first to break away.

"Believe it, beautiful, and you did it." Airy tucked his hands in his pockets, fighting the urge to grab her and press his lips against hers.

"Hey, if you don't mind, I'm kind of new. My boss wants to come by and snap a few pictures of my work for my portfolio.

I told him I would, but he's anal about making sure everyone meets *his* standards," the graphic artist stated.

"Yeah, that's fine." Nixie shrugged as she and Airy walked into the building and back to where her office was. The furniture had arrived the day before, and Airy made sure to assist her with getting it together and hanging her art on the wall. "I never got to thank you for helping yesterday, hell, helping me every day."

"No thanks needed. Getting to spend time with you is thanks enough."

"I do need to thank you, Airy, because you don't have to do this, but I appreciate it." She took a seat behind her desk while Airy took the one directly across from her. "I know I've been taking you away from work, and the women who fall at your feet have got to be upset that you have spent all of your time with me." Airy released an arrogant chuckle.

"The only woman I care anything about how they feel is you."

Nixie shut her eyes tightly in an attempt to stop the rapid beating of her heart. Swallowing hard, she slowly returned her gaze to him. Airy's stare was so intense it caused her to take in a sharp breath before slowly releasing. Her pussy was leaking and eager to unite the two of them, but she refrained from giving in.

"You haven't even known me that long, Airy." It had only been a month since they met in his office, but they talked or saw each other every day. Feelings were definitely developing, and it wasn't just one-sided.

"You're right, but every day, I'm here with you. Every time we talk, I learn a little more. Every day, I'm more and more intrigued in everything involving you."

"I've *still* got a boyfriend."

"You think I give a fuck about that?" Airy scoffed and ran his hands down his face. He was trying to find a way to express what he wanted to say without being brash, but it was harder than he expected. "You don't even like that nigga." He released an aggravated chuckle. "Even now when you just said you had a boyfriend, all of the passion and desire left your tone. That in itself says a lot, Nix."

"My mom says the same thing." Nixie chuckled, thinking about the conversation she had with her mother and sister. "It's just so hard to throw away three years." She sighed.

"You're thinking about love like it's measurable, and that's your first mistake. Love is not about quantity. It's not about how many years but the quality of those years. If he doesn't ignite something in you so powerful that leaving him wouldn't even be a second thought, then maybe you should rethink the quality of those three years."

The night she left her sister's house, when she got home, Adam had a nice candlelight dinner set up for the two of them. They sat down and had dinner and then had sex. It was the most awkward sexual experience in her life. There were no feelings from either side and nothing that made her believe that leaving him wasn't the best thing for her. Still, he tried, right?

"I don't want to talk about this." She ran her hands

through her curly mane and laid her head back against her headrest. She could feel Airy's stare on the side of her face, but she opted not to look his way. "Airy—"

"No, I get it. I overstepped. I told you that I would give you time and space to figure shit out, and I'm a man of my word. I just hate to see you put yourself through this, and you don't have to."

"No, I just—"

"No need to apologize, baby." He held up his hands, eager to change the subject. No matter the words that were coming out of his mouth, he felt an insane pull that led straight to her, and he didn't know how much longer he could deny it. "So tell me about your company. I know you make all-natural products for the skin, but what's the process?"

"You don't want to hear about that. No one wants to hear about that." She giggled nervously. Adam's voice rang loudly; it was very rare that he allowed her to talk about her business, so she usually kept it to herself and reserved it for conversations with her mother and sister.

"Don't tell me what I do and don't want." The confidence in his tone cut through the room like a knife. "I'm a man. If I didn't want to know, I wouldn't have asked."

"I'm sorry, I just—" she started, but he cut her off.

"You have so much to learn about fucking with a real nigga." Airy smirked then kicked his feet up on her desk, while crossing his arms across his chest. "Can you tell me about your business without the extra commentary?"

Nixie's mouth opened and then shut. She was trying to

find the words to say, but Airy was making it extremely hard. Her eyes met his, and it was like time stood still. Her breathing picked up speed, and her heart battered her rib cage. Their lustrous moment was interrupted by a knock on the door.

"How can I help... Devon?" Nix stared into the eyes of her ex-boyfriend. She didn't know if she wanted to throw her paperweight at his head or just ask him what the hell he wanted so he could be out of her presence.

"Aye, Nixie. I didn't know this was your building." Devon smiled and ran his hands across his freshly lined fade.

"Funny, the name on the building says *Nix Beauty*." She crossed her arms across her chest and shook her head. "Just like the graphics that I ordered, but I'm guessing that's why you just had to come over here and check on your employee." The snide look on his face had her leaning toward tossing the paperweight in that moment.

Airy watched the exchange between the two of them, and just like when she was arguing with Adam, he could feel her disdain for the unwanted visitor. The feelings burrowed in his belly as anger crept through his veins.

"Oh, I'm sorry for being rude. My name is Devon. I'm the manager at Just Like That Graphics, and me and Nixie used to date right out of high school." He smiled like it was something to be proud about.

When he stuck his hands out toward Airy, he just looked at him, not bothering to return the gesture. Instead, he turned his attention toward Nixie who wore a scowl on her face. Their eyes met, and they shared a little nonverbal communication before Nixie shook her head and smiled at him.

"Is there anything I can help you with, Devon?"

"Nah. I just wanted to come and let you know that everything was done, and my guy did an amazing job."

"He really did, and I'll be sure to leave a positive review. Now, you can go." Nixie's tone was sharp and quick. There was no need for pleasantries, and she wanted him out of her line of sight.

"Why so harsh? I thought we ended amicably." He couldn't even hold the lie himself before he burst out laughing like he had just told the funniest joke.

"Devon, you were a little boy trapped in a man's body. You weren't ready to settle down and used the relationship I had with my mom and sister as your reasoning for not wanting to be with me anymore, and that was okay. That was one fuck up I was glad to get rid of." She smirked, drawing a chuckle from Airy.

It was an inside thing from the first night they met. He was low key digging the fact that she remembered and wanted to address it, but the unwanted guest decided he wanted to linger.

"Can we help you with something, my nigga?" Airy stood, slipping his hands in his pockets.

Nixie watched as Airy took charge of the situation, and she had to admit it was sexy as hell. She wanted to jump on him and ride him till the sun came up. His tall chocolate frame was in defense mode and was daring Devon to say the wrong thing.

"My bad. I didn't know you were her guy. I thought she was still with the Adam dude. No disrespect."

"Don't matter who the fuck she's with. The lady has showed you on more than one occasion that she didn't want you here, but yet, here you are. If there's nothing else, you can get the fuck out before I become a problem for you. Don't let the suit fool you or get you fucked up." His tone was even yet confident, smooth yet powerful, and it damn sure had Nixie's panties soaking wet.

Devon chuckled as he took a step further in. He was a macho dude, ego was bigger than his personality, so the thought of being threatened moved him, just in the wrong direction this time.

"I get it, the pussy good, but I promise you, it ain't worth the headache. Wait until you meet her bitch of a mother and sister. Those bitches stayed in our business and made my life a living hell. Every time she gets pissed, that's the first place she gon' run, and they fight her battles, all of them. So, you ain't getting just one bitch, you getting three." Devon laughed.

Devon was a cheater, and he didn't have too much going for himself back then. They shared a few years together, and every time he would hurt Nixie, she vented to her mother and sister, who automatically rallied around her. Even after Nixie forgave him, Natalia and Navi didn't, which caused friction whenever they were around each other. That coupled with the fact that he didn't respect her enough to keep his dick in his pants, their relationship seemingly died, but clearly, Devon still felt a way about it.

The sound of Devon's cackling infuriated Nixie to the point where she indeed picked up the paperweight and launched it at his head, which halted all sounds of laughter.

"You stupid bitch!" he growled, but before he could even take a step in her direction, he was hit with a right to the face, which stunned him for a second. Devon hadn't had a fight since high school, but he hadn't forgotten how to get down. It was just too bad he was no match for Airy.

"So, you hit women, muthafucka?" Airy growled as he delivered powerful blows to his face and abdomen. Nixie flinched every time his fist connected; it was like he broke bones with every hit.

"Airy, that's enough. He gets the point." Nixie shook herself out of her initial shock and made her way around the desk. "Baby, please, that's enough."

Hearing her call him baby instantly snatched him out of his fit of rage. He blinked a few times before he turned to her and then slammed Devon by his shirt on the ground. He went to her and looked her over as if she had been hurt when his hands were the ones bleeding.

"Damn, the pussy got you going all out. 'Bout to get your ass locked up for that thang, huh?" Devon taunted as he tried to pull himself off the ground.

Hearing his voice caused Airy to black out, but Nixie jumping in front of him brought him back to reality. His chest rose and fell as he sent daggers in Devon's direction.

Bringing him to his reality, he was in a room with a man who almost tried to kill him and would have had Nixie not stepped up in.

Deciding to take his loss, he turned and limped out of the office. Airy turned his attention back to Nixie and made sure that she didn't have a scratch on her. He knew that he didn't give Devon a chance to get near her, but he still had to make sure.

"Baby, I'm good. You sit down and let me clean your hand." Nixie tried to walk him over to sit him down, but he shook his head.

"Nah. First I'm going out there to make sure that he's gone, and then I'm calling my security guy to get you some cameras in here. I don't trust that pussy."

"Devon ain't gon' do nothing. You bruised his ego and beat his ass. He'll go telling the world that he got jumped to make himself look bigger and badder than he really is, and he'll make sure to keep his distance. That's who he is. Hell, I could have beat his ass myself." Nixie smirked.

"Damn, babe, you really know how to pick them." Airy furrowed his brows before a smirk spread across his lips.

"Oh, shut up." She laughed and followed him out of the room. When they got out there, they noticed that white paint had been splashed on the windows and a black Ford F-150 was spinning out of the parking lot. "I told you he was a bitch." Nixie growled. "I was going to do my grand opening next month, now look at this shit."

"I'll have that cleaned up and replaced by tomorrow." Airy

walked over and locked the door to the shop and headed to the back where his phone was.

He busied himself getting someone here to clean her windows and make sure that her logo and other window art was fixed. Even though she said that he wouldn't try anything, Airy wanted to make sure that she was safe, so he put in a call to the security office as well.

"Let me clean your hand," Nixie said as she sat on the desk in front of him and reached for his hand.

Airy knew that he said that he would give her time and space, but he had to follow his heart, and it was telling him to make his move, and he did. Grabbing her by the waist, he pulled her down so that she was on his lap. He just knew that she was going to move or offer up a lecture about her boyfriend, but instead, she smirked and started working on his hand.

He watched as she cleaned, disinfected, and bandaged up the cuts he had due to connecting to Devon's mouth. The delicacy of her movements did something to him. It lit everything that he was trying to suppress. The way she was taking care of him because she thought he was hurt, fed his heart, and now he needed to return the favor.

"There, all done," she said, looking over her shoulder.

The smile that had graced her lips was welcoming, but one look in his eyes, it quickly turned to lust. Tucking her bottom lip between her teeth, she tried to talk herself out of what was about to happen next. She couldn't, and if she had to be honest, she was tired of fighting the feeling that burned between the two of them.

"Please stop looking at me like that, Nix."

His words hung around the lust filled air as they both battled internally with the inevitable. He knew what he wanted. He just didn't want her to have any regrets. Once they crossed that line, things between them were going to be different. He was ready; he just didn't know if she was.

Airy's warm minty breath brushed against her exposed shoulder as a low and pleasant hum slipped her lips. Her body yearned to be touched, pleased in a way that she had no knowledge of. She needed to feel wanted, appreciated, and even though validation wasn't a necessity, she wanted it and with Airy.

He's gonna think you're a hoe.

Who gives a damn!

Throwing caution to the wind, she leaned down and pressed her lips against his, allowing the kiss to linger, which was a clear indication that she wanted everything that had crossed his mind.

"Listen, Nix, once I get started, that's it. Things will never be the same, so don't let this moment dig a hole that will later be filled with regret. I want you so fucking bad right now, but if you're not one hundred percent ready for me, then I'm man enough to take a step back until you are. You let me know how you want to play this."

His brown eyes bore into hers. She tried to think of any

reason she could to remove herself from the situation, but she didn't find not one. Her willpower had lost the fight, and her flesh had gained control over her conscience. Her body and her heart wanted Airy, and today, she was letting them both have their way.

Without saying a word, she stood from his lap and turned so that she was facing him. Reaching for the hem of her shirt, Airy held his hand up to stop her. Standing from the chair that he was sitting in, he made a few short steps in her direction.

Nixie's heart pounded hard as he finally came to a halt right before her. Her gaze traveled up his tall, lean frame until her eyes met his. Smirking, Airy leaned down and pressed his lips against hers.

"Nah, the fucking pleasure is all mine." He winked, grabbing her hands and placing a soft kiss on her them before tugging at the hem of her shirt and pulling it over her head.

He dragged his tongue across his lips when he saw that she was braless. His dick didn't even give him time to process the thought before he climbed to his fullest potential, pulsating against the fabric of his Tom Ford slacks.

Looping his index finger in the waistband of her wide leg dress pants, he worked it around until he stumbled upon a zipper which he quickly undone. He didn't want anything in the way of his prize. A lustrous grunt rumbled through his chest as he lowered himself to the ground, assisting in removing her pants from around her feet.

Airy trailed a heap of light kisses up her thighs, leading to her pulsating center. Dragging his lips across the thin lace of her thong had her fighting the moan that was trying to escape. A rush of pleasure jolted Nixie fiercely, sending a wave of light shivers through her body.

"Shit!" managed to escape through the sea of obscenities that were swimming around her mind.

Heat sizzled through her when she felt his fingers slide her thong to the side. Her clit jumped with a rush of lust that left her gasping and throwing her head back the minute his thick, wet tongue traveled the length of her slit.

"Fuck this," he groaned. With one swift motion and a sudden *pop,* Nixie's thong was now in two pieces and on the ground. Her brows furrowed at him as he made his way to a standing position, but before she was able to say anything, he had her back against her desk and her legs opened wide and his tongue around her clit.

"Oh shit." She gasped as she tried to lean up to look at him, but the way she was positioned, her head was hanging over the desk and her legs were pushed back to her chest.

"I knew yo' ass was gone be something fucking special. It don't make no fucking sense for pussy to look, smell, *and* taste this fucking good." Airy mumbled against her center before diving back into his new favorite meal.

Circling her clit with his tongue, he watched as it stiffened a little more and slightly jumped at his touch. He could tell that her pussy had been mistreated, and it was a damn shame. Good thing he knew just what to do to fix it.

Pleasure trickled down every nerve ending that Nixie possessed. Things were twitching and tingling that she didn't know could twitch and tingle, sending her core into a frenzy. She shook her head back and forth desperately trying to think clearly, despite the satisfying sensation he was delivering, but all that she could come up with was, *damn this nigga a beast*!

"What the fuck!" Nixie swallowed hard as she wound her hips in his direction, offering him more of her.

"That's it, baby. Feed ya man, shit."

Slipping two fingers into her pussy, Airy groaned against her clit, drawing a few crazy sounds from Nixie. Her sexy cries and the way her pussy wrapped around his fingers had his dick aching to be free and inside what he had already deemed *home*.

"Airy, shit, that feels a-fuckin-mazing! Shit." Her tone was lust filled and breathy.

With a crooking of his two fingers, he found her spot, the spot that caused her to wiggle underneath his tongue. The spot that sent her heart rate on a race while her breathing fought to catch up. Her legs took on a light tremble, making him smile on the inside. He was starved for her, and nothing would satiate that need but her release.

So fucking sexy. Shit!

Airy watched her squirm and felt her attempt to smother him with her thighs, but he didn't care. He was almost to the place that would give him the most satisfaction, and he wasn't about to let anyone stop him, not even his ringing phone.

"That's it, Nix. It's right there, baby. Let it go," he coached.

Her pussy muscles clamped around his fingers as her legs

shook violently. She was on the verge of a powerful orgasm, and he couldn't wait to witness it. Latching onto her clit, he sucked while simultaneously exploring her spot with his fingers.

"Oh God! Oh shit! Fuck! Fuck! Fuck! Airy, baby, yes! Abso-fucking-lutely yes," she moaned, throwing her hips into him.

The orgasm tore through her center, sending her nerves into a dancing frenzy and her stomach in knots. Unadulterated bliss covered her as she tried to bring herself back down from the high she was on. It felt like she was floating almost, like an outer body experience.

"So fucking beautiful." He slowly removed his fingers and Nixie suddenly felt an emptiness that she needed fulfilled, and he was the only one qualified to do it.

"I want to feel you," Nixie moaned, grabbing her hardened nipples and massaging them between her fingers. "Like now." She gave him a look that told him waiting was not an option, and Airy was not there to disappoint.

Grabbing her by the thighs, he pulled her to the edge of the desk so that her ass was slightly hanging off. He held her up with one hand while he used the other to disrobe from the waist down. Once he had worked his way out of his pants, he leaned over so that he could press his lips against hers.

"You sure about this because a nigga is gone off the taste of your pussy. So I know when I cross this threshold, I won't be able to control my actions when they come to you. Be sure this is what you want."

"I said now." Nixie moaned with no hesitation, bringing a chuckle to Airy's lips.

Placing the head of his well-endowed dick at her opening, Nixie leaned up when she felt the first sign of pressure. When her eyes landed on his dick, a shocked expression registered that quickly turned into admiration, landing on desire. Pulling her bottom lip between her teeth, she moved her hands so that she could balance her weight on them. There was no way she was going to miss what he would do with that third leg.

Big dick fucker.

Airy delivered slow yet powerful strokes, giving her more of him little by little. He watched as her beautiful face contorted into everything that she was feeling at the moment. There was pain mixed with pleasure, but not one minute did she look as if she wasn't having the time of her life, and that's all that he wanted.

"I fucking knew it." Airy cursed himself for taking it there with her. He knew that he was low key starting to fall for her, and now he was wrapped around her perfectly manicured fingers. "Got damn," came through clenched teeth.

"Airy, yes." Nixie's harmonious moans floated through the air.

Airy could feel himself about to explode, and he didn't want that. Quickly pulling out, he caused Nixie's eyes to pop open. His absence sent a wave of sadness that she knew would be an issue for her, but she couldn't deny that it was there, so when her eyes met his, he smirked. He, too, felt the same emptiness.

As he dived back into her again, pleasure threatened to drown him and take him to the place that he was forcing himself not to go.

"Your pussy is so wet, Nix. You know that?"

"Baby, it's wet for you," she moaned, reaching up to pull him in for a kiss. "You got my body lit. I don't know if I'll ever co-come, umm, shit, down from this high. Oh God!"

"Grip my shit, girl," he teased as she looked down at his dick covered in her juices. The sight was beautiful and belonged on a tape of some sort, but being embedded in his brain would suffice. "I swear your pussy feels like home, baby. I could live in this shit."

"Ummm, fuck, Airy. Show me then," she challenged.

"Say less." He placed his massive hands on the back of her thighs and sped up his strokes. The sound of her sopping core echoed through the room as they both began to grunt and moan. "Like that, baby?" Airy said through clenched teeth.

"Shit, it's deep! Fuck, baby. Ah, yes. I feel it, baby." Her head was thrown back, and her eyes were shut tight as she prepared her body for another gut-wrenching orgasm.

"Got damn. I think I love this shit."

"Best dick ever." Nixie's eyes popped open momentarily because she thought she said that in her mind, but it definitely found its way through her lips.

Airy chuckled as his thumb found her clit, bringing out a slew of obscenities.

"Fuck, Nix, you gripping." Airy had half the mind to pull out again, but her pussy had a good grip on him as he continued to paint his name on her center. He wanted to make sure that she never forgot this moment, but what he didn't know was he had made an impression on more than her pussy.

"Shit, Airy, fuck me! Yes, baby!"

"You like that shit, huh?"

"I'm about to cum. Shit, I'm about to cum."

"Nah, I need you to hold that."

"Baby, I can't, please." Her whine sounded like she was on the brink of tears and caused Airy's dick to jump within her.

"Come on, baby girl. Hold that for me." He slowed down a little and started grinding into her while applying the perfect amount of pressure on her clit.

"Oh fuck!" Her legs started to tremble, and she began to throw her pussy against him, matching him thrust for thrust. "Ummhmmm, baby, I need to release thissssss, shit!"

"Damn, you gon' make me bust, baby. Come here." He pulled her up and placed his lips against hers as he continued to grind into her, and she matched his thrust. "Cum with me, baby. Fuck." He parted her lips with his tongue as they moved in sync with the melody of their love sounds.

The moment was damn near magical as they both were whisked away in a sea of pleasure and bliss. The stars aligned in the moment, and they both felt like they were floating as they connected in a way that neither of them could have ever imagined.

"Shit!" Airy hissed as he thrusted inward, filling her

waiting womb with as many of his seeds as he had to offer, and Nixie happily obliged.

"Oh. My. God." She threw her head back, giving Airy the perfect access to her exposed neck. Latching on, he sucked gently as they both came down off of their mind-blowing high. "Wow." Nixie moaned when she felt his member throb inside her, prompting her pussy to react.

"Shit!" Airy hissed.

Nixie's eyes opened as the reality of what just happened settled around her, searching for the guilt or regret of her actions, but neither registered within her conscience. Not that she would have cared in this moment anyway. No man had ever taken the time to explore her sex the way that Airy had. She wouldn't say it out loud, but Nixie was hooked. She was already planning when she would see him again in her head.

"Wow!" was all that she could think to say. Airy chuckled and pecked her lips, allowing the kiss to linger.

"You said that already."

"I don't think there's enough wows in the world to completely describe how you made my body feel. Like, I'm speechless, and I'm never that. It's like I'm in fear of saying the wrong thing and not giving what you did the justice it deserves. Got damn it." She threw her head back, and Airy laughed, bringing her stare back to his.

"The feeling is mutual." He kissed her again.

Their eyes met, and they had an unspoken conversation. They were so into it and only broke the silence when there was a knock on the door up front. Looking at each other, they both frowned and let out groans as Nixie finally released his semi hard dick from her hold.

Yep! She's home!

Airy could feel his dick getting pissed at him already, but there was nothing that he could do at the moment. Whoever was at the door was banging like a maniac and showed no signs of letting up.

"Expecting company?" Airy asked with a brow raised.

Nixie furrowed her brows at him and then looked at the clock. "Ugh, yes!" She shook her head and then walked to the bathroom that was connected to her office. "My sister is supposed to meet me to look at the graphic designer's work. She was thinking about upgrading her graphics."

Airy laughed as he leaned against her table, looking at his phone that was going off. He saw that it was Kawan. "Well she won't want nothing from him, I'm sure."

"Nope! Hey, all I got in here are feminine wipes, but you're welcome to come wipe down. I do have a pack of new toothbrushes in here. I figured I'd be spending a lot of time here, and I hate not brushing after I eat, so you're welcome to one."

They both walked into the bathroom and cleaned up. Airy had the urge to take her again, but when both of their phones started ringing, he knew that it wasn't an option. Once they were cleaned up and dressed, minus Nixie's panties, they walked back into her office.

"My sister is cursing me the fuck out." Nixie giggled.

"I'm guessing Kawan is with her because I've been at least six muthafuckas."

Nixie sighed.

"Any regrets?" Airy held his breath waiting for her to answer as he silently prayed she said no.

She slowed her pace and turned to him; he couldn't read her expression. A knot formed in his throat. He tried to swallow it, but it wouldn't budge. When she stood on her tiptoes and kissed his lips, she smiled.

"Not a one."

"Good, because I'm trying to be inside of you by the end of the night."

"I'm definitely good with that." She chuckled right before someone began to bang on the door, when they both turned to look at a pissed off Navi and Kawan.

"Come open the damn door, nasty asses!"

Chapter Nine

LESSON 9

Love Doesn't Play The Victim

"I was starting to think that you forgot about your old man." Senior slowly opened his screen door before he surveyed the happenings up and down the street of his home. Once his evaluation was complete, his focus returned to his only son.

He lived in the same house that he raised his son in, refusing to move with the thought that somehow, he wouldn't forget the memories that were made before everything went downhill. This was his home, the home that he built for his family. How could he ever let this go?

"How could I ever forget about my pops? You're all that I got." Adam's tone was dry. He wasn't in the best of moods. He had been calling Nixie all day, and every call went straight to voicemail. He was aggravated and felt disrespected at her lack of caring about his feelings, and the minute he saw her, he was going to make sure that he told her just that.

"I can't tell. It's been weeks since I saw you."

"Pops, I just brought you dinner the other night," Adam said, sliding inside the door that his father held open for him to enter.

"That's different; you dropped off food. You didn't bother to stay and hang out with your old man." He huffed.

Senior was spoiled when it came to his son's time. He needed to hang with him at least once a week and talk to him every day. Adam was the only thing that he had in his life that he felt he could count on. His ex-wife showed him that not all love was unconditional, and he counted on his son to make him feel different.

That wasn't really fair to Adam, but he did what he had to do because, at the end of the day, outside of Nixie, his dad was all that he had.

"My bad. Nixie and I had plans," he lied. Nixie had been keeping her distance outside of the one night they actually had sex. Things felt different, physically and emotionally, but he counted it as she was doing too much with her *little* business.

Senior grumbled a few things under his breath before he shook his head and turned to walk away. Heading into the living room and taking his seat in his favorite chair right in front of the TV, Senior blew out a hot breath at the thought of Adam blowing him off for time with *her*.

"How are things with you and Nixie?" he asked, not really

wanting to hear what he had to say but just starting up conversation.

"Not so good as of lately. That's why I didn't stay the other night. I wanted to get home and try and have a talk with her. All we've been doing is arguing about the dumbest shit." Adam threw himself in the recliner that sat adjacent to his father. "I just don't know exactly what to do to make her see what I need her to be for me."

Saying it out loud allowed Adam to hear how selfish he really sounded. Even though the realization hit him like a ton of bricks, he couldn't stop the way he felt.

"When they get like that, then you go out here and find a pretty little thing, spend some quality time with her, and then throw it in her face. That's what's wrong with women today; they think they run shit. It's up to you to show them that they don't. As soon as she realizes that you can move on from her, she'll shape up." Senior smirked. "I should have done that with your mama, and maybe things would have ended different."

Adam mulled over his words for a second before his loaded gaze fell on his dad again. His heart thumped against his chest at the thought of not having Nixie in his life. That's not what he wanted. What he did want was for her to realize that she was the woman and he was the man. That dynamic was important to him and his sanity, and she didn't seem to give a damn, and that's what pissed him off the most.

She wanted to be independent, wanted to own a business and become famous for it. That wasn't ideal in Adam's world.

He knew firsthand what happened when women got a little hint of power: they ran with it.

When he met Nixie, she worked a corporate nine to five. Once she was off work, it was him and her. He loved that; it's what he wanted in his life. They had money and time for each other. She played her part as his woman, and he felt like a king. All that changed when she started the *stupid* skin care line.

Time became scarce, conversation changed, and the way people viewed her changed which in turn made her attitude change. At least that's the way Adam saw it, and he didn't like it.

"Ummm, I don't think that will work with Nixie." Adam chuckled under his breath. "Her flippant mouth and eagerness to make sure she knows her worth—she'll drop my ass like a bad habit, and I'm not sure if I'm ready to let her go." He sighed. "I just hate that we argue all the time."

"What ya arguing about, son?"

"Her business." He rolled his eyes to the sky and ran his hands down his face. "She feels that I should support her like she supports me, but she doesn't understand that I work to make sure that she can have her little dream," Adam lied. There was no way that he could let his father know that her business was taking off, and she could hold her own with or without him. "She thinks that I should be there at every turn, but what she doesn't understand is that without me working, we would sink."

"You should have left that girl when she dropped that

corporate job. I told you that it was a mistake. She reminds me so much of your mother." Senior ran his hands across his freshly cut salt and pepper dark fade. "I don't want you to go through what I went through, son. Building your life with a woman only for her to break it off and take off because her career is more important than her family. That's a different kind of hurt, son."

"I know, Pops. I was there. Through it all, I was there with you."

"That's why I don't understand why you stick around. Your relationship mirrors what you saw me go through. Why put yourself through that, son?" Senior sat up in his seat and turned his head so that he was looking in his son's eyes.

"I love her and—"

"Love don't mean shit! Love will have you crying over someone that didn't think you were good enough to stay home and take care of a son that you helped create. Love will have you wondering where the hell you went wrong. Love will have you hating the person you thought you loved. Love will ruin your got damn life. Mark my words."

Senior threw himself back in the chair and shook his head. He hated that he was still bitter about Adam's mom leaving them when she got a little bit of fame, made a little bit of money.

"Let me tell you something." Senior huffed and cleared his throat as he continued. "My mother and father, God rest their souls, were together for fifty plus years. All because my mother knew her role as his wife. Were they happy all the time? Probably not, but it worked because everyone stayed in their place. If you want a long-term relationship, make sure your requirements and expectations are known now. Don't let her get too far away from what *should* be."

Definitely too late for all of that. She's so close to opening her store.

"I hear you, Pops."

"Don't hear me, son. I'm telling you; your mother is a prime example."

"Speaking of her, she called me. Evidently, she's in town and has been for a while." Adam cut his eyes at his dad as he held his breath, waiting to see what he was going to say. Normally, he would be yelling and screaming about him staying away from the woman who brought him into this world, but right now, he couldn't even read his expression, prompting him to speak again. "Did you hear what I said, Dad? I said that my mo—"

"I heard ya!" he snapped, taking Adam aback.

"I'm sorry, I just—"

"Just do me a favor. Don't speak her name in this house. She doesn't even deserve the energy it takes you to speak it or me to hear it." He placed his hands on the arms of the chair to assist him with standing, and he headed for the back of the house. Before he completely disappeared, he turned to his son and said, "Let yourself out."

After all of these years, he was still bitter; everything surrounding his ex-wife bothered him to a point where he couldn't focus, or think, or... anything. He couldn't do anything. Depression crept into his heart, and seeing her just the day before didn't help at all.

She showed up out of nowhere and placed him in the worst mood. Hearing his son talk about talking to her pissed him off more than he cared to admit. So instead of giving in to a screaming match about how much of a selfish *whore* his mother was, he just cut the conversation short with his son. He would make it up to him later when they talked.

"What the hell just happened?" Adam sat looking around the now empty living room. He wanted to go back and ask his father what that was about, but he thought better of it. Instead, he stood and made his way to the door, shaking his head. He would have preferred his father to curse and scream instead of walking away from the conversation.

Adam felt bad for his dad. He had seen him depressed over his mother leaving. He had seen him raging because she wanted to come back. He had seen the worst of the worst, and he knew that he didn't want that for himself.

Maybe my dad is right... about everything.

Sighing heavily, he walked out of the door with a heavy heart and the fate of his relationship heavy on his mind.

———

"Got damn it!" Nixie yelled as she dropped the bowl of face cream on the floor.

She had just mixed a new product that she had tried a couple of weeks prior, and she had planned to launch it at her grand opening. Her goal was to have at least one hundred made and bottled before then, but her dropping product wasn't leading her to meet that goal.

Heading to the back, she grabbed the products that she would need to clean up her mess and then she made her way back into the kitchen. Her phone chimed as she was about to get to work. When she picked it up, she couldn't fight against the smile that made its way onto her face. A feeling of excitement stirred in the pit of her stomach as she thought about the pleasure he laid into her.

What the fuck is he doing to me? she thought as she read the text he had just sent, a few times.

I'm eating this steak and I swear all I taste is you... could just be in my head though

Her bottom lip slipped between her teeth as she thought about the words that seemed to dance across the screen. At that moment, she didn't know if there was an explanation for what she was feeling, but she couldn't escape, and to be honest, she didn't want to.

That could be your senses telling you they miss me 😊

Oh, bitch, you just bold now, huh?

A lust filed giggle rattled her chest as she thought about what she typed before she hit send. Shaking her head at herself, she looked at Airy's name flashing across her screen. Not wasting anytime sliding the green answer button, she smiled when his chocolate face appeared on her screen.

"Yo, don't do that shit," were the first words out of his mouth, sending Nixie into a fit of laughter. "Shit ain't funny.

I'm trying to respect the fact that you have to handle your little *situation* still, but you saying shit like that could fuck all of that up. You know that, right?" His right brow hitched.

Airy bit down on his back teeth, causing his masculine jawline to flinch, driving Nixie crazy in the process. A soft moan slipped her lips inadvertently, and Airy didn't miss it. He smirked at the notion that she felt the same way he did. Respect for other people's relationships had been something that his parents had taught him, and he was trying, but the more he absorbed the passion that lived in her orbs, the harder it became.

"I'm just saying, Airy Menz, you started it." She winked, trying to recover from the open invitation to her thoughts that she had offered up.

"I'm more than prepared to finish it." Silence flooded the line as they both just stared at each other. Nixie bit down on her bottom lip, thinking if she could actually get away. Then she groaned.

"I can't!" She sighed and then turned the camera around, doing a sweep of her kitchen and dining room and then of the mess she had on the floor. "That's what I was doing when you called. The grand opening is coming up, and I wanted to launch a new product at the same time."

"Shit! I'm sorry! I forgot all about that." Airy was kicking himself for interrupting her when she was trying to work. "You told me that the other day. My bad."

"It's okay. I just—"

"It's not okay, Nix. The last thing I want to do is to interfere with what you have going on. My goal here is to assist in your elevation, not to distract it. So as much I want to use my tongue as a sexual weapon, I'll use my thoughts and memories until you're free to satisfy my urges."

His eyes were low like he had been smoking, and his tone was laced in lust. That had her attention, but what caused her to have to clench her legs closed was the beautiful smile that spread across his face, exposing thirty-two perfectly white teeth. Again, she moaned.

"Damn it, Airy," she whined, bringing a low and throaty chuckle through his lips.

Airy watched as Nixie alternated between pouting and biting her bottom lip. He was so in tuned with her every move... the way her shoulders hunched when she was trying to decide whether to be an adult or not. The way her body tensed when she, what he assumed, was squeezing her legs together.

He didn't blame her, because he was sitting behind his desk with his dick in his hands. Everything about this woman was sexy. Even the fact that he couldn't see her at this moment because she was building her business, was intriguing to him.

"I'm sorry, baby, but I tell you what. As soon as you can find a minute or take a break, just call me. I'm gonna shoot you my address. I have to show a couple of buildings then I'm calling it a day."

"Good luck on your day. I hope you get a really big sale. That way you can take me on vacation." Nixie attempted to lighten her mood. Even though she would rather be riding Airy to sleep, she knew that she had work to do and a conversation to have with Adam.

"I don't need luck when I got skill." He popped his collar.

"The arrogance is oozing." She rolled her eyes, making him chuckle.

"Well when you know what you can do..." His words trailed off as his lustrous gaze said that he meant that in more than one way. Nixie groaned. "Aight, I'm done fucking with you. Get back to work, baby girl, and if you can get away, hit me up, and I'm all yours."

"Airy." She whined as a smile tore across her face.

"What?"

"You know what! But let me go. If I can get at least twenty bottles filled and ready to go, I'll be okay, and I'll hit you."

"Sounds good, baby. Be easy."

"Is it bad that I don't really want to say bye?" Nixie looked down before her eyes found the screen again. "This is so weird. Just a little while ago, I was content with my life and my boyfriend, and after one meeting with you, you got me rethinking everything I thought I knew. That's so fucking crazy to me."

"Why?"

"Why what?"

"Why is that crazy to you?"

"Because I—I just feel this crazy connection to you, something that I've never felt before, and the shit is bugging me out." She spoke nothing but honesty. "It's like I'm ready to throw away three years of what I know for the unknown, and what's even more crazy is that I'm not even scared about it."

"That should tell you right there that what you *had* was never what you thought it was. He doesn't feed your soul, he doesn't nourish the seeds that he planted, he doesn't make sure that you have what you need to be the woman that you were destined to be. When you don't have that... that connection from the soul, it's easy to lose sight of love."

"I guess you're right. Adam was always a this is what we need to do, and this is what needs to happen so we can get where he thought we needed to be man. He doesn't believe in dreams or women who chase them. That's his problem with me. When we met, I worked for Duke Energy, nine to five, Monday through Friday. I felt like I was suffocating, like I was in a box and couldn't get out."

"Did you talk to him about it?" She nodded and moved her eyes from the camera. "And what did he say?"

"He said that that was the way of life, it's what you were supposed to do when you became an adult. More bullshit he learned from his father. He said the money was good, and it would be a mistake for me to leave. And this was after I had started my skin care line and it was doing really good." Nixie sighed.

"He didn't want to see you grow. Outgrow him." Nixie nodded in agreement. "He was scared of your potential. That maybe, just maybe, you would see that he wasn't the man that he was pretending to be all these years." Again, she nodded. "Why?"

"Why what?" Nixie's eyes cast down to the ground.

"Look at me, baby." His tone danced around the kitchen and landed right on her heart as she did what she was told. "He knew that you were too good for him the minute he laid eyes on you, but he put on a front. A front that got you, but the minute you were ready to spread your wings, his bullshit started to show, and that's okay. Just don't let his insecurities stifle the person you were meant to be."

She didn't even know that she was crying until she felt the warm wetness on her cheeks. What he was saying was true, all of it, every single word. The only reason she stuck around was because she did love him and the fact that she knew what he went through with his mom leaving and the poison his dad pumped into him. Nixie felt sorry for him, but she didn't know if she could do it anymore, not at the expense of her happiness and sanity.

"See, there you go about to make me say fuck yo' little *situation*. I don't like to see you cry except for when I'm too deep and it's feeling that good."

"You know what..." A smile took over the somber look that had plagued her face, and it made Airy smile.

"That's my girl. I couldn't get off this phone with you feeling all sad. Just hurry up and come see me." He winked.

"Okay." Nixie ran her hands through her curly hair. "Let me get this mess up and get to work."

"Sounds good, beautiful. I'll see ya later."

"Okay." Nixie smiled and went to hang up the phone, but

Airy called out to her instead. "Airy, don't say anything that will have me fighting against hanging up this phone."

He chuckled. "I'm here if you need me, aight." Nixie nodded with her lip between her teeth. "And stop doing that shit; you got my dick hard as fuck right now."

"Bye, Airy." She hung up to the sound of him laughing through the receiver. "That man."

For the next two hours, Nixie whipped and mixed to the sound of Beyoncé. She had all of her music in a playlist, and she just put it on shuffle. After she met her goal of the twenty bottles of face cream, she looked at the time and felt like she had time to whip up enough product for twenty more so she could be ahead of the game.

She took what she had made and placed it in the extra bedroom that she used for storage. She loved the three-bedroom single family home that she purchased right out of college with the help of her mother and stepfather. One of the rooms was used for when Adam pissed her off, and the other consisted of all of her stuff for her skin care line, all the products that she'd made and bottled for her opening. Nixie couldn't wait to be able to move all of this over to her store which should be in a week or so.

Grabbing what she needed, she headed back in the kitchen and began to whip up a new batch of her new face cream when "Dangerously in Love" started blaring through the speakers. There was a time when she would sing this song with so much conviction and passion, but it didn't have the same meaning anymore.

Adam wasn't the same man anymore, and she was hating herself for not acting on it sooner. The changes happened right before her eyes, and she didn't do anything to stop it. That was her fault and hers alone. She knew what she was dealing with, and she had met his father and listened to his *views,* but she thought her heart was big enough to make him see different.

It was the same thing with Devon. Nixie knew she had a thing for fixing broken men, but now it was affecting her happiness and her business, two things that she couldn't afford to lose.

"Why do you have the music so loud?" Adam walked in with a scowl on his face. "You can hear it all the way outside."

"Umm, because I was working and wanted to listen to music." He had fucked up her mood that fast. Sighing heavily, "Hey, Adam. How are you? How was your day?" she snidely replied.

"We have neighbors. Did you think about them?" Adam didn't know why he was being so snippy with her. She hadn't done anything to him, but his conversation with his father was heavy on his mental. "All I'm saying is you could have shown a little more consideration to them."

"That's funny because the Raineys are out of town, and Ms. Morton is at the hospital. I know this because I actually talk to the neighbors you all of a sudden care so much about." Humor and sarcasm laced her tone, further aggravating Adam.

"I'm glad you think this is funny. You won't when you get a noise ordinance."

"Yeah, I'm pretty sure I can't get a noise ordinance for a house *I own*." Nixie made sure to annunciate the I and the own. "I'm not sure what the fuck happened before you got here, but I suggest you go and figure that shit out because I haven't done a got damn thing to you." By now, Nixie's hands were on her hips, and her angered glare was locked and loaded. If looks could kill, Senior would definitely be planning a funeral.

Adam ran his hands down his face, and he looked at Nixie's angry disposition, sighing because he knew that he was the one that instigated the tension between them. Now it would be harder to have the conversation that he needed to have with her.

"Look, I just wanted to have a conversation with you real quick about us." She mumbled something under her breath before she turned her back and began to work. That infuriated Adam. "That's the damn problem, Nixie. You don't respect me as the man in the relationship. You think you run shit, and you don't. My father was right, you—"

"Ah, that's what this is about." Nixie released an aggravated chuckle while shaking her head back and forth. "I'm not doing this with you. I'm actually over doing this with you. Every time you leave your father's house, you come back on some bullshit, and I don't have time for it. You let him poison your thoughts if you want to. That shit has nothing to do with me."

"That's why our relationship has went to shit! You never have time for me anymore. Everything is about your stupid ass business." Adam was trying to calm himself, but he just couldn't. Every time Nixie opened her mouth, it enraged him even more.

"So, all of our relationship issues are my fault? Wow, okay, cool!" Nixie chuckled, but there was nothing humorous about it. She told herself not to say anything else, but she wouldn't be her if she didn't. "Why is my business that big of a deal for you? You would think that a man would want his woman to have some business about herself, yet you're intimidated by it."

Adam scoffed. "I'm far from intimidated, sweetheart. I'm just tired of coming second to something that will never amount to shit." His harsh words caused Nixie to take in a sharp breath and slowly turn his way.

"What the fuck did you just say?" Her head cocked to the side as she narrowed her eyes at him. "Are you for real right now? Like really fucking for real?"

"As real as I can be!" Adam shook his head and crossed his arms across his massive chest. "I'm sick of all you talking about and thinking about is this bullshit." He waved his hands in the air.

For a while, Nixie didn't respond. She didn't move. She just stood there looking at him. There was no way that this was happening right now, at this moment. She had to be getting punked or something.

"Thank you, Adam. Thank you." She winked and grabbed

her things and took them back to her storage room. She thought that maybe she would be pissed or ready to knock his head off, but honestly, she was relieved. He had just made this so much easier. Granted, she was wrong for cheating, but right now, she didn't care. It was time for her to live for her and be happy, and none of that included Adam.

Chapter Ten

LESSON 10

LOVE IS AN ACTION, NOT JUST A FEELING.

"Where can and can't I sit, hoe?"

Navi walked around Nix Beauty with her nose turned up. She remembered the last time she knocked on the door, and she was met with a freshly sexed face sister, hair all over the place and disheveled clothes. She wanted to make sure that she didn't land her ass in lustfully made passion juice.

"Stop being dramatic, Navi." Nixie giggled and rolled her eyes playfully. "*We* thoroughly cleaned, and then Airy hired a cleaning crew to stop by too."

"*Airy hired...*" Navi mocked and batted her eyes in a taunting way. "The way you say his name lets me know that the dick is worth talking about." Navi threw herself on the sofa that lined the small waiting area, quickly jumping back up before drawing an ugly scowl from her sister. Navi laughed before slowly lowering herself back onto the sofa, opting to put her hands in her lap, *just in case*. "So, tell me, little sis, how did Devon busting up in here being a bitch end with you on Airy's dick?" A snide smirk slid its way on her sister's lip.

"Bitch, you assumed I was on the dick, but until you have proof of said sexual acts, then I's innocent." Nixie winked and continued to move boxes around. She had just gotten a shipment of products that would grant her the opportunity to start making her products there instead of at home.

Navi jumped up and dramatically swung her hair over her shoulder and placed her hand on her hips. "You can't even say that with a straight face."

Nixie bit down on her lip, attempting to halt the smile that was breaking away. The fight was a no win for her because, before she knew it, she was doubled over laughing.

"Why you questioning me like you didn't show up interrupting what I had going on?" she got out between giggles.

"Because I didn't get the scoop, because Kawan ass told me to mind my damn business. And lucky for you, I decided that I didn't want to fight with my husband *that day*." She waved her sister off. "I could literally smell the sinning through the door. Yo' ass got tore out the frame, and it showed. Hell, it still shows." She moved her hands the length of her sister frame.

"Maybe because that wasn't the last time." Nixie mumbled

and shied away from her sister's shocked expression while suppressing another smile.

"Bitch, you better spill." Navi lowered herself back down on the sofa, getting comfortable. "And don't leave shit out, and hurry the hell up because you know Natalia's nosy ass is on the way." Navi playfully rolled her eyes.

"You better stop talking about my mama, Navi."

"Stop fucking stalling, Nixie Land."

"I mean, there is nothing to tell. After Devon's bitch ass came in here showing his ass and Airy stepped up in my honor, everything in me felt like it was set on fire. My heart wouldn't allow my mind to think of anything else except for climbing his tall, chocolate ass." Her shoulders shook from the memory of the things that he had done to her. "I don't know, Navi. The feelings that I have when I'm near him is like some supernatural force yanking me by the soul and dragging me into his arms. Even when I'm fighting like hell. You ever feel that shit?" Nixie's loaded gaze fell on her sister.

She knew she sounded crazy, but that was the only way to describe what she was feeling when it came to Airy. It didn't make sense, and it honestly scared the shit out of her, but oddly enough, she welcomed it.

"Sounds like you've met your soulmate, sissy pooh."

"What?" Nixie narrowed her eyes at her sister, waiting for the punch line, but when none came, she thought about the words that left her lips. "I—I..." She shook her head in an attempt to free her thoughts and feelings, but they were bonded, wrapped up in a nice little chocolate bow. Nixie sighed.

"I felt the same way with Kawan." Navi's dreamy eyes and the smirk on her face let Nixie know that she was thinking about her husband. Nixie didn't bother to interrupt her thoughts; she loved her sister and brother-in-law's relationship. They were the epitome of black love, and she was definitely here for it. "I fought so hard against it, so hard that I almost lost him to my resistance. I was so caught up with not being like Mom that I almost missed out on the best thing that ever happened to me. Don't let certain *circumstances* keep you from your happiness. I've been there. Hearing Mom's story and seeing what she did in a different light shows that she's been there, and you, Nixie..." she stood and took her sister's hand, "...you've been here, in this dumb ass relationship with this dumb ass nigga for way too long. It's time for you to be happy."

Tears welled up in Nixie's eyes because she knew that her sister was right, but there were still some reservations about her feelings for Airy. The first being she thought that everything was moving a little fast; however, she damn sure wasn't pressed to slow them down, but that didn't stop her anxiety about it.

"I really like him, Navi. Like, he makes me feel things mentally, physically, and emotionally. That fine, tall ass, chocolate ass, broad shoulder having, solid frame, seductive eyes ass—"

"Got damn, Nixie. You got me all hot and shit from you

just talking about him. Shit, tell me more." Navi placed her elbow on her knee and propped her chin on her hand as she gave her sister her undivided attention.

Nixie furrowed her brows, and her eyes turned to slits; she gave her sister a look that one on the streets would have taken offense to, but instead, Navi just laughed.

"Bitch, I will—"

"Don't blame me. You sounded like one of them author chicks writing about them men in them sexy books. Shit, you had me all the way in. I wanted to know more." She laughed.

"Whatever, hoe! Don't make me call my brother."

"Call his ass. I don't care. I ain't fucking with him today." She rolled her eyes and sat back on the sofa and pulled out her phone. When she realized that she didn't have a missed call or text from Kawan, it kind of made her a little sad, but she wasn't about to dwell on it. They would talk about it later; they always did.

"Don't you start. You were just in la la land, thinking about him, and now you mad. What happened?"

"Nah... you trying to deflect. This ain't about me, hoe. This is about you and your whorish ways. Mama should be ashamed." Navi threw her hand on her heart and clutched what would be pearls if she were wearing any.

"Says the queen of deflection." Nixie rolled her eyes and opened another box. "There is nothing else to tell. I like him, a lot, and I just met him. That scares me." Nixie sighed heavily before returning her focus to the contents of the box she had just opened. "On top of trying to sift through those feelings, I'm still dealing with the bullshit with Adam." Nixie sighed again. "It's just a lot."

"But you don't have to be dealing with that, Nix. You *choose* to still deal with him."

"What do you suppose I do, Navi? Walk in the house and tell him to get the fuck out because I found someone who believes in me and values who I am as a woman? Someone who actually listens to me and what I want and need? Someone who knows *exactly* how to make my body succumb to him in ways that should be illegal?" Nixie tucked her bottom lip and lightly bit down.

"Got damn," Navi whispered, whipping out her phone and starting to type a message before she decided against it and dropped her phone back in her lap. Her focus returned to her sister who was delivering the evilest glare. "Bitch, what?" She threw her hands up. "Shit, you were doing that romance shit again." She rolled her eyes. "But yes!"

"Yes what?" Nixie's face grew tight.

"That's what you should do!" She stood and walked over to the counter and leaned her back against it. "Walk in the bitch and say, aye, my nigga, your time has expired. Your boss has been digging my guts out, and I can't get enough of that shit."

"Naviiiiiiiii." Nixie whined before her face broke out into a smile. "You're not helping me."

"I just told you what to—"

"I am not doing that, it would—"

"Not doing what?" Natalia walked in looking like she had just stepped off a photo shoot for an international magazine.

She walked over and kissed Nixie on the cheek before she did the same to Navi, then brought herself back in front of her two daughters. "What were y'all talking about?" She placed her purse on the table beside her.

"Nosy ass." Navi mumbled under her breath.

"Um, and where are you coming from looking like star?" Nixie placed her hands on her hips and smiled at her mother, attempting to interject the standoff between Natalia and Navi.

"Stan and I did lunch, but enough of that. Stop deflecting. What were y'all talking about? It must have been important. Y'all didn't even hear me come in, and, Nixie, the look on your face said that your sister was giving you horrible advice."

Natalia cut her eyes at Navi, who she needed to have a conversation with, but it could wait until they were alone. She knew that her daughter hated for people to be in her business, even though she found herself in the middle of everyone else's.

"Nothing. I'm trying to find the perfect way to break up with Adam. I'm seeing more and more that he is not the one for me. There is nothing that I can do to try and fix this, and I'm tired of trying, if I have to be honest. I just-just want to be happy, and Adam is not that for me. He needs to do some soul searching on his own so he can be a better man. I'm just not trying to stick around through that process."

"What brought on the sudden change of heart?"

"Airy," Navi choked out. Both Nixie and Natalia glared her way. Navi only smiled.

"It's not really sudden, Mom. I..." Nixie ran her hands through her curly hair before crossing her arms across her chest. She sighed. "I see what you have with Stan and what Navi and Kawan have. I guess I wanted that too. It just took me a while to see what I was losing to obtain it. I see it now."

"Baby, Stan is a man that I prayed to God for. After being with your father for almost twenty-five years, I knew that when I finally broke free, I wasn't settling for anything less than happy. I don't want that for you. I don't want twenty-five years to pass you by before you finally realize that you deserve to be happy. But let me ask you a question. Do you love him?"

"Who?" Navi and Nixie said at the same time.

"Adam, who else?"

Navi giggled while looking at her sister who threw her a bird.

"Umm, I have love for him. I mean, how can I not. We've been together for three years, but he doesn't light my soul on fire, Mommy. He doesn't give me butterflies, and my heart doesn't race at the thought of him or his touch or his kiss."

"You're doing it again." Navi's sing song tone had daggers shooting her way, but she never looked up from her phone to see them. Natalia sighed, not even willing to give her oldest the energy.

"I just don't feel that with him," Nixie whined.

"Do you feel guilty about it?"

"Would it make me a horrible person if I said no?" Her eyes closed as she took in a sharp breath and then released it slowly before she began to speak again. "Adam is so stuck in his ways that anytime I try to insert myself or my love, he shuts it down. It's been that way since I started Nix, but I can't sacrifice my dreams for his ego."

"As you shouldn't!" Navi finally gave her sister her attention. "Fuck him!"

"Navi! Language!" Natalia scolded. "And since you got so much to say, let's talk about why I got a phone call from my son-in-law this afternoon?"

"Whelp! That's my cue." Navi stood up, grabbed her purse and her keys, quickly kissed her sister and mother, and then headed for the door.

"That's what I thought." Natalia chuckled while shaking her head. "We will be having a conversation about this."

"I'll see y'all later." She threw her hand up right before the door shut, and Nixie and her mother were left alone to bask in her absence.

Natalia watched as her daughter strutted down the sidewalk and then around the building. She never turned her attention until she was no longer in sight. "I'm not really sure what to do with that one."

"Um, Mom, you should know by now that all you can do is love her." Nixie chuckled and continued to move through the boxes that were delivered earlier.

She was hoping that the conversation that they were just having was over, but she should have known better. She could feel Natalia's eyes on her, but she tried to busy herself with unpacking her things. Knowing it wouldn't last long, Nixie used what little time she did have to attempt to piece together her thoughts.

"Tell me what's going on, Nix, because up until the other day, I didn't really know things were so bad with you and Adam." She took a seat at the desk that sat at the front and turned toward Nixie.

"I wasn't trying to pull y'all into my drama again. You know how things went with Devon. I knew that if we fell out and I forgave him, y'all wouldn't. So, I dealt with it myself to avoid unnecessary tension."

"Devon is a little ass boy trapped in a man's body. He wanted to keep living his high school years well into his twenties, and no one had time for that. He needed to grow the fuck up, and when I see his funky breath ass, I'm gonna tell him just that. Little fucker."

Natalia got mad all over again. When Nixie called and told her that Devon tried to attack her, she wanted to call his mama and tell her what a piece of shit she raised, but she decided against it, telling herself that she would most definitely see him again, and she couldn't wait.

"I know that, Mama, but I still involved y'all in my bullshit and just kept running back to him, thinking he would change. It's my fault he said that stuff."

"It is not your fault; that was all him!"

"Well that's why I kept all of that to myself. Whenever Navi complained about my relationship, I would just silently agree or make excuses, but I'm tired. I want to be happy, and I'm not happy with Adam."

"Then break it off."

"I am. It's just whenever I go to have that conversation, we argue. Then I'm all pissed off, and you know how I get when I get mad. Things will come out all wrong, and I'll end up looking like the bad guy for telling the truth about how I really feel. I want to do this while we're both calm in an attempt to get him to see things the way I see them. I'm not what he's looking for, and he's not what I need." Nixie sighed. "I wish I was cold hearted enough to send a text message."

"That's the thing, baby. No matter how you look at it, you're going to be the bad person. There's no way around that because he's going to see you leaving him as betrayal. You have to realize his thought process has nothing to do with you. How he feels about you after you break it off is no longer your concern. However, right now, you're playing with his feelings because you're giving him false hope that there is still something with the two of you, and there isn't. Do the right thing and break it off. And don't you dare send no text. I taught you better than that. Treat people good..."

"No matter how they treat you." Nixie finished her sentence and shut her eyes tightly.

A small slither of guilt tried to make its way in her heart because her mother was right. She was playing a dangerous game. She should have broken it off with Adam long before Airy crossed the threshold of her greatness. She groaned inwardly, knowing what she needed to do.

"Now, tell me about this Airy character." Nixie swallowed hard. "Don't act like I didn't hear Navi. This is the third time

I've heard his name, so I know there's something there, so you may as well go ahead and spill it."

Nixie's tongue glided across her now dry lips, and she tossed her curly mane over to one side. Her eyes danced around the shop as she thought about the pros and cons of telling her mother about how she really felt about Airy. Her mother wouldn't judge her sudden shift in male focus, but she would want details, details that Nixie didn't know if she was ready to share.

"Airy is a... *friend*."

"Since when do we start lying to each other, young lady?"

Natalia could see the battle in her daughter's eyes, a battle that she was sure to take a L on when it came to their open relationship. They were all close, and Natalia knew that she inserted herself a little too much, but it was never in an unhealthy way. Just more so letting them know that she was there for whatever, and they could confide in her.

"Mommy, I really like him, like a lot. He's so in tuned with who I am as a person and woman. He supports every move I make and encourages me when I doubt myself. He's like my best friend with some damn good benefits." Nixie's eyes stretched wide when she realized that she had just revealed more than she wanted to, but the damage was done, so she went with it. "Sorry, Mom, but this man makes me feel things I've never felt. Things with us happened super quick, but I don't regret it."

Natalia smiled at the conviction in her voice. If she was

speaking that way, then she was way more invested than she led on.

"How do you think Adam will feel knowing that you pretty much cheated on him? Because that's the truth of the matter. Even though you're unhappy and you want to break things off, you haven't; your commitment is still to him. So, you're doing the same thing to him that Devon did to you, and that's not fair, Nix. I know what it feels like, and it's not a good feeling. You need to handle your business." Nixie groaned and mumbled a few things under her breath. Her mother was right, but it was just so much easier to just pretend like Adam's feeling weren't valid, but they were. "Don't mumble. You know what I told you. Don't open one door until you close the other..."

"Because eventually, they'll collide." Nixie rubbed her temples as she finished her mother's sentence. "I know, I know, it's just... just... I don't know. It's like every time I go to have the conversation, we start arguing and then I—"

"You don't want to have the hard conversations, but it's necessary, Nixie. You're wrong, baby girl. Don't be like me. Let that man go so that he can start his healing process and possibly get to where you already are. If you keep this up, it's going to blow up in your face, baby. Mark my words. Before you get too involved with this man, end things with Adam."

I'm already too involved.

Sighing, she opened her mouth to say something, but the door to her shop chiming, signaling that someone was walking in, got her off the hook, or so she thought.

"Saved by the... Airy, what are you doing here?" Alarm was evident in her tone, and Airy picked up on it quickly, like he did with everything that had to do with her. His eyes shifted over to the older version of Nixie and Navi and then back to the woman he came to see. Knowing she didn't have any other choice than to introduce them, she lowered her head and swallowed hard before doing the inevitable. "Mom, *this* is Airy."

"Nice to meet you, Mrs....?"

"You can call me Natalia." She smirked and held her hand out, in which Airy brought it to his mouth and placed a soft kiss on her knuckles. "Okay, Nixie, I see why you're so smitten with this man. Handsome, and he comes bearing gifts."

Nixie groaned at the smirk that spread across Airy's lips at Natalia's admission. He was glad to hear that she felt the same way he felt, even though he was way beyond *smitten*.

Natalia crossed her arms across her chest as a pleased smirked rested on her beautiful face. Nixie shook her head at her mother before she finally focused in on the beautiful bouquet of flowers and box that he had in his hands.

He's so got damn sweet.

"It's a pleasure, and I sure see where she gets her good looks from." Airy winked, laying on the charm.

"And a charmer. Umph!" Natalia smiled and then turned toward her daughter. "We'll finish this conversation later, maybe over dinner one day this week," she said in a way that didn't give Nixie very much room to decline. "And, Mr. Airy, you're welcome to join us." She nodded.

"I would love nothing more than to get to know my future mother-in-law." Airy smiled, bringing a sharp breath from the pit of Nixie's belly.

She could feel her mother's eyes on her before she heard the amusement in her voice. *"Friends, huh?"* She laughed and shook her head. Nixie completely avoided eye contact with both Airy and her mother.

"Nix has been through some things, one of those things she's dragging her feet to *get rid of*. I know that she doesn't believe in fate or the stars aligning and all that good stuff, but what I need her to believe is that I'm not going anywhere, so she should just get used to it."

Nixie's eyes leveled with his as she searched them for something that looked or felt like deception, but there was none. He meant everything that he said, and that had her tingling from her head to her feet. This man was everything, and she was ready to receive him, as soon as she released herself from her baggage.

"I like him, Nix. A man that knows what he wants is my kind of man." Natalia nodded as she walked over to where her purse was and slipped it on her shoulder. "Dinner, this week." She pointed at Nixie who rolled her eyes but nodded, and then she turned her attention to Airy. "Mr. Handsome..."

"Mommmmmmm," Nixie whined.

"Hush, chile." Natalia waved her off. "I'm going to let you

know now, I don't play about my baby. She's a good woman with a big heart, and she deserves the world—"

"And I plan to give it to her, if she lets me." He was speaking to Natalia, but his eyes never left Nixie's. She could feel the confidence in his tone, and her heart fluttered. When his eyes landed on Natalia again, a pleased smile was across her face, and he knew that he had won her over.

Like mother, like daughter.

"Well now that we got that out of the way, I hope to see you at dinner sometime this week. Family is very important to me, and if you're going to be a part of that, I'd like to get to know you better."

"Absolutely! It's a must that we all get acquainted." He smirked. "I'll definitely be seeing you soon."

"Well, I'll let you two be." Natalia kissed her daughter on the cheek before offering up a hug for Airy, which completely had Nixie in shock. Once she was gone, the two of them sat in silence for a minute, both tucked away in their own thoughts.

"She likes you."

"Who doesn't?" Airy's left cheek hiked, placing a lazy grin across his face, right before his tongue swiped across his bottom lip, making Nixie clench her legs together.

"Arrogant ass."

Running her hands through her hair, Nixie cast her eyes down to shy away from his intense stare. That on top of the black tailored Tom Ford suit that wrapped his body like a glove had her hormones out of whack and her juices flow-

ing, and that was the only way to control what she was feeling. His chocolate skin glowed under the dark fabric,
bringing attention to his handsome face. The man was *fine*,
period.

Airy closed the gap between them and pulled her to him.
Feeling her breasts pressed against his chest had his dick
rising to the occasion. The smell of her fruity perfume had his
heart battering his rib cage and him feeling the need to
connect with her. So, he did.

"Damn, you smell good." He whispered as he tucked his
nose into the crook of her neck. "Shit!"

His plan was to come and hand deliver flowers and a small
gift before heading to show his next property for the day.
Nixie had the kind of pull on him that whenever she was in
his presence, she pulled him out of his reality and into hers. In
a way, that caused him to lose his sense of time, something he
never had an issue with before.

It was crazy that she had so much power over him, power
that he willingly handed over with the notion he wouldn't get
her heart in return. He was almost there with her; he could
feel the wall that was built around her heart slowly making its
way down, gearing him up to be right there to swoop in and
protect it.

"So do you. What are you doing here?" she asked as he
pulled away and placed the flowers in her hands.

"Since when do I need a reason to come and see your
beautiful face?"

Nixie blushed, biting down on her back teeth. She shook

her head at him. "You know what I mean, Airy, and these are absolutely beautiful. How did you know?"

"When I say that I want you and want the best for you, I'm not just talking, Nixie. I mean that shit. And I make it my business to match my words with my actions." He winked. "I said that to say, I listen to everything you say. Your words and your actions show me who you are and what you need from me, so I listen." Airy leaned in and placed his lips against hers and allowed them to linger.

A soft moan escaped her lips as Airy engulfed her small frame into his massive arms. His hands slowly dipped down to her lower back as he pulled her into him as close as he could get her. When her tongue slipped between his lips, he knew that he had to interrupt their moment because if he didn't, he wouldn't be making it to his meeting or anywhere else.

"Damn it, Nix." He pulled away and adjusted himself in his slacks. "You don't know how bad I want you right now. I want to bury my face in your pussy until you cry, and then make love to the very spot I attacked. Damn it."

"You gotta showing, so I need you to stop talking like that. Gon' have me in my office handling myself." She smirked.

"No! Hell, I'll cancel first." Airy went to reach for his phone, and Nixie burst out laughing as she grabbed his hand to prevent him from making the call. "You are a mess, you know that?"

"Nah, what I am is serious as fuck."

"I know, and that's what makes it funny." She stood on her toes and placed a soft kiss on his lips.

"I need to see you tonight." Airy damn near begged, causing Nixie to groan and roll her eyes.

"I can't," she said barely above a whisper. "I have to go and handle this situation with Adam."

"Now that I won't stop you from doing." Airy kissed her lips and then took her hands in his. "If shit pops off or he even looks like he's about to start some shit, I'm one fucking way. Matter of fact, do you want me to come with you?"

"Um, I don't think that will be a good idea." She giggled nervously. "Adam's not like that though. He'll say some mean things, but that's as far as it will go. I'm sure of it."

"I don't really trust that, but I trust you, so just know I'm a phone call away. Matter of fact, text me one letter, and I know that I need to make my way to you."

"You don't even know where I stay, Airy."

"You don't know what I know, and on that note, let me get out of here. I've got a new client that I need to get to, and hopefully, I'll see you later, right?"

"Let me see how this goes." She leaned up and kissed him again.

"I promise to make it worth your while."

Nixie shivered at the thought of what that could possibly mean, softly moaning into his embrace. Resisting this man was damn near impossible, so she was already trying to make plans to get to him later that night.

Chapter Eleven

LESSON 11

Love Is Not Happiness.

Airy checked his phone to make sure that he had the right time and building. His client was late, running close to an hour, and he was slowly losing his patience. He couldn't help but to think of the fact that the time he was wasting waiting on this mystery client, could have been spent with Nixie.

He was already annoyed that the client requested a viewing under a company name and not the name of the actual client. Typically, he would pawn a showing like this off to a newer agent, but the request came in directly for him. *CDM Agency.* Airy read the name on his calendar again before he released a frustrated sigh and walked around the spacious office building.

Kawan had secured the office building from his client Charles which placed 108 single office spaces on their listings.

Each office space had an office with a door, a small waiting or receptionist area, and a personal bathroom. It was sure to bring in quite a bit of money, and the company couldn't be more excited. Airy was first up for the sale, if his client ever got there.

His phone vibrated, and he looked down and saw that it was his mother. Smiling, he slid the button across to answer it.

"'Sup, Ma?"

"Don't you, ''sup, Ma' me. Why haven't I seen your face?" Anna fussed on the other end of the phone. She was pissed that she hadn't seen her son in weeks. Yes, he had called, but she wanted to see him.

"I'm starting to think you just like fussing at me." Airy chuckled.

"You must think this is funny."

"I'm sorry, Ma. I've been busy with work and trying to figure out things with the beautiful Nixie Land. I can't wait for you to meet her; you're going to love her." Airy smiled at the thought. "She's snappy like you, and she has a smart mouth. She reminds me so much of you."

"What you trying to say, Airy Menz?" Humor laced her tone, giving Airy the okay to chuckle.

"Nothing, negative lady. I just can't wait for you to meet her."

"How old is she?"

"Really, Ma?"

"Yeah. I don't trust you after that thing you brought to my house the last time."

Airy groaned at the thought of Constance. She was the last person that he wanted to talk about or see. She had still been on her bullshit, calling and texting. Had even popped up a couple of times, but he refused to let her in.

The last time she showed up, Airy stepped out onto the porch and warned her to stay away from him. That was the last time that he heard from her, and that was two weeks ago, and he was happy. He damn sure didn't want to talk her up.

"Nixie is nothing like her. She's twenty-nine, no kids, she owns a house, and runs her own business."

"Okay, so what's wrong with her?" Anna asked, feeling like there was a but somewhere in the mix.

"Nothing, other than she has your *pop off* tendencies." He chuckled. "Seriously, she's amazing and beautiful. She has this energy about her that makes you want to be in her presence. From the first time I saw her, I knew that she was *the one.* You always told me that when you know, you know, and I do."

"I can't wait to meet her, son. She sounds amazing, but back to me not seeing you. Make that shit happen, Airy, soon!"

"Yes ma'am. Let me go. I think I hear my client walking through the doors."

"Okay, son. I love you, and this week!"

"This week!"

Airy chuckled before hanging up the phone and slipping it into his pocket. He took the short hallway that led to the entrance of the office building. The company wanted to look at a space on the top floor.

"I'm so sorry I'm late."

The minute Airy heard that voice, he bit down on his back teeth. Pissed was an understatement because, at this point, she was trying him. Airy did his best to contain his anger, but people like her made it hard for him.

"Why the fuck are you here?" he asked through clenched teeth, slowly spinning around to face a smiling Constance.

She was dressed to kill in a black bondage dress that hugged her hips and laid right above her knees. The six-inch peep toe heels made her appear taller than she was, and they added to her sex appeal. Her beautiful light brown eyes and long sandy hair made her look so innocent, but Airy knew better.

"You like what you see?"

"What. Are. You. Doing. Here!" Airy made sure to enunciate every syllable in hopes that she understood that he wasn't fucking around with her, and she was about to see another side of him, which she picked up on almost immediately.

"I'm here to see a property for my company. I'm starting a publishing company that helps freelance writers connect with the right people. I'm going to offer editing and proofing, and I'll be like the agent. Like the middleman that places them in the center of success."

"Congratulations, and I'm proud of you." Airy sighed, knowing that she was on some bullshit, but he was trying to give her the benefit of the doubt. "Cool, so you want to look at a space on the ninth floor. Elevators are right this way."

He knew that he probably should have refused to work with her, but he had never been one to turn down money, and he wasn't about to start. He would just have to keep his guard up around her. Once she signed the paperwork and it was listed as sold on his site, that was going to be the extent of their business relationship, and he would make sure of it.

Chuckling to himself, Airy had to give it to her though. She went to great measures to be in his presence. She knew that if he saw her name that he would have declined the meeting, and she didn't want that.

"Thank you, Airy. That means a lot." She moved in for a hug, and he stepped out of the way.

"Not that kind of party, Constance. This is business, and we can treat it as such, or I can leave, and you can find someone else to sell you an office space. Your decision."

Sighing heavily, she rolled her eyes and threw her hands up in surrender. Airy nodded and turned toward the elevators and pressed the up button. When it came open, he stood back and allowed her on first, and then he stepped on and pressed the nine.

"Ever the gentleman."

"Despite how I feel about you, my moms would cuss me out if I did anything other than the gentleman thing." He glanced her way before focusing on the numbers that were above his head, signaling what floor they were passing.

"The gentleman thing to do would be to take me in this elevator and make me remember who you are, Airy Menz."

"You're too fucking old to be playing these games,

Constance. I should not have to fucking explain to you why I don't want you. You should know. These little pop ups and bullshit you trying are on my last nerve, and I won't say what will happen when I'm all out of patience. Tell me now, either you trying to see this space, or I can walk your ass up out of here, and you can figure this shit out on your own. I don't want you! I don't want anything to do with you! We will never be anything!" Airy glared down into her eyes in hopes that she saw just how serious he was. "I'm done fucking with you. I'm done being fucking nice!"

"I—"

"Nah, if what you're about to say doesn't start with *I get it, Airy* or *I'm done with the bullshit, Airy*, then don't say shit, and let's end this meeting now. You need to decide if dick that doesn't belong to you is worth fucking up the business you're trying to build, if there even is a business."

"I have a business, Airy. I wouldn't lie about that."

"Aight then, cool! What's it gonna be?"

Sadness lingered in her eyes, but Airy had no sympathy for her. The minute she thought it was okay to go and kill his seed without him knowing killed anything that he could ever feel for her again. She needed to understand that, and the sooner she did, the better off they would be.

Sighing heavily, Constance stared at Airy as the elevator doors opened and then shut again. She could see the disdain that he had for her in his eyes, and it hurt her heart that he didn't see her the way she wanted him to. She missed Airy, most of all she missed what he could do to her body, but he wasn't budging. At least not today.

"Who is she?"

"You really think I'm fucking with you." Airy reached over and pressed the button that would lead them back to the lobby.

"There has to be someone that would make you not even want me anymore. I mean, look at me." She looked down her body as she held her hands out as if she was offering herself up to him on a silver platter. "There was a time that you couldn't keep your hands off of me."

"There was a time that I could trust you; that time has lapsed. Get over the shit and move on because I have."

"So, there is a she?"

"Goodbye, Constance. Don't fucking contact me again!" Airy said as he pointed to the opened elevator door.

"Listen—"

"Get the fuck out, and don't contact me again."

"Okay! Okay! I get it, but I really need an office space."

"Call back and reschedule with someone else. I'm done, and I mean that shit."

Constance opened her mouth to say something but decided against it as she lowered her head and headed for the exit. He was really done with her, and there was nothing that she could do about it. Sighing heavily, she shook her head and left. The offer in California that she was offered was looking better and better. Airy was the only reason that she wanted to stay, but he had drawn a line in the sand, and she needed to accept it.

"I really did love you, Airy," Constance said once she reached the door.

"You had a really great way of showing it, Constance. Goodbye."

Once she was gone, Airy leaned against the desk and ran his hands down his face. He was beyond annoyed and wanted nothing but to lie between Nixie's legs. Pulling out his phone, he shot her a text.

What I would give to be laying between your legs right now.

Not even about sex... just the peace of being close to you!

Sighing, he slipped his phone back in his pocket, but as soon as he did, it vibrated, letting him know that Nixie had responded.

At the hospital with Adam

Dad had a heart attack... I need your energy right now too!

See you later.

Airy didn't really know how to feel. The fact that Nixie was being there for Adam rubbed him the wrong way, and then on the other hand, he knew her heart and how caring she was when it came to others. He would look at her different if she wasn't there for him.

Then his mind drifted to thoughts of her hugging him while he cried on her breasts, the same breasts that he loved to pull between his teeth and suck until she hissed. That had his anger rising, but he couldn't be mad.

We're not together... Yes, the fuck we are!

Don't be letting that nigga touch on you. He can cry by his got damn self.

Airy thought of his words as being jealous and on the childish side, but he didn't give a fuck. He meant what he said when he said that Nixie was his, and that was the end of that.

Jealous much?

Airy chuckled at her response and thought about his words before he typed them out.

I've never been jealous a day in my life... until I met you!

The thought of anyone getting remotely close to what I've experienced drives me fucking insane! So yeah you can call me JEALOUS!

He watched as the bubbles appeared and then disappeared. This happened a few times within a few minutes with no response. Right when he was about to place it back in his pocket, he got a response.

I don't know why that crazy shit just turned me on!

Airy burst out laughing before placing his phone back in his pocket. He was satisfied with the thought of her thinking about him while she was with Adam. The fact that she took the time to text him back made his heart smile.

———

"I'm glad you can smile at a time like this." Adam cut his eyes in the direction of Nixie. He was pissed that his father was in surgery and no one was telling him anything. He didn't mean to take his frustrations out on Nixie, but at the moment, she was the only one there. "Must be important for you to be focusing on that instead of my father, who's having a life-threatening surgery right now."

Nixie rubbed her temples as she tried to soothe the frustration right out of her brain. The reality of the situation was that she didn't even have to come. There was no secret that Senior didn't care too much for her and would probably be worse off if he knew that she was there. She shook her head at the thought because she had never done anything to the man other than inform him that he couldn't talk to her any kind of way.

"Should I leave?"

"What? That's what you got out of what I just said? That I want you to leave?" Adam's brows bunched together, eyes cut into slits. "If you don't want to be here, then just say that."

Nixie couldn't believe his tone. She wanted to spaz, but she knew that he was hurt behind his father, and she was doing everything in her power to keep her composure. However, her patience was running thin... really thin.

Without engaging him, Nixie rolled her eyes and brought her attention back to her phone. She wasn't about to feed into Adam's bullshit.

Would I be wrong if I tell this nigga I don't want his ass while his father is fighting for his life? Yeah, that would make me like a super bitch, huh?

She snickered at the thought while scrolling through her social media, anything to take her mind off of her current situation. She could feel his eyes on her, but she was not about to allow him to ruin what had been a pretty good day. Then again, every day had been a good day since she'd been with Airy.

"Family of Adam Leary, Sr.," the doctor stated as he came through the doors of the waiting room. Adam stood immediately, but when he realized that Nixie wasn't standing with him, he gritted his teeth and then shot an angry glare her way.

"Nixie!" Adam scolded as if she were a toddler touching something that she shouldn't have.

She had to laugh to herself to keep from giving him the business that he was so close to obtaining. Slowly rising, she stood beside him while crossing her arms, silently cursing herself for even showing up for him, something that he had never done for her.

Once she was by his side, Adam looked at the doctor and nodded for him to continue.

"Mr. Leary is a strong one; he suffered from a mild heart attack. We put a pacemaker in. There was some damage to one of the valves in his heart. He's going to have to eat better and take better care of himself if he wants to live." The doctor looked back and forth between Adam and Nixie. "I'll refer a cardiologist and a nutritionist for him. We'll keep him here for a few days for observation and then he'll need someone to stay with him for a while."

"Of course!" Adam shook his head. "So, he's going to be alright?"

"With some medication, healthier eating, and exercise, yes; he should make a full recovery."

"Oh, thank God. Thank you, Doctor."

"Pleasure is all mine. Now, if you'll excuse me." He nodded and turned to walk off.

"Wait, can we see him?" Adam blurted out.

"The nurse will be in to take you back. He's really weak right now and needs his rest, but you can see him for a bit."

Once the doctor walked off, Adam released the breath that he didn't know he was holding. Emotions took over him, and out of nowhere, tears fell from his eyes. Nixie had never seen Adam cry before, and she instantly felt like shit for the feelings that she was having.

"It's gonna be okay, Adam. He's gonna be okay." She wrapped her arms around his neck and allowed him to cry on her *shoulder.* "I'm glad he's okay," Nixie whispered, comforting words into his ear as they stood in the center of the waiting room, embracing.

Moments later, the nurse came back and instructed them on where to go. Nixie had planned to let him go back and she was going to head home and get more work done, but the way he grabbed her hand didn't allow her to.

Walking in the room, the smell of ammonia hit them in the nose almost instantly. The sound of beeping took over their sense of hearing, and Nixie felt bad all over again when she heard Adam's soft cries, until...

"What you doing all that crying for?" Senior's tone was hoarse and low, almost like it hurt him to talk.

"You scared me, Pops," Adam said, letting go of Nixie's hand and taking the seat next to Senior's bed. "You're the only thing I have left in this world. You're the only person I can count on. If I lose you, I'll have nobody."

Well what the fuck am I? Nixie thought but opted not to say anything. They were done anyway; what he thought she was or wasn't in his life was of no concern of hers, but hearing that just put the last nail in the coffin. She didn't mean anything to him. She was just something that he could claim, a trophy if you will. He never saw her as a life partner, and that was okay. She felt the same way.

"Ya damn right, I'm all you got. She sure as hell ain't gon' take care of you. Too busy worry about building herself up to think about you. I swear you made a huge mistake when you..."

"Nixie, I think it's best you just leave." Adam interrupted his father.

Nixie tilted her head and stared at Adam like he had sprouted two heads. Not only was she pissed and two seconds from flipping on the both of them, she couldn't believe that Adam sat there while his father spoke to her the way he did.

"Wow!" Nixie pulled herself from the wall and headed for the door.

"Good riddance!" Senior called out as soon as she opened

the door, causing Nixie to pause and snap her neck his way. "You were never good enough for my son. I can't wait until he wakes up and realizes just how much you are like his mother."

"Yeah, well I'm about to be more like her than either of you know," Nixie sassed.

"Nixie!" Adam said through gritted teeth.

"No. Don't Nixie me, Adam!" She shook her head. "We need to talk ASAP, so meet me at the house." She gave him a knowing look and then shut the door and headed home.

Adam wanted to go after her, but he felt like his dad needed him more. Nixie would just have to be okay. What his dad said wasn't completely off base. She hadn't been the woman he needed as of lately. All of her time and energy went to Nix Beauty, and if he had to be honest, he was tired of it. She needed to make a decision and fast.

"The biggest mistake you made was leaving your wife for that woman," Senior announced.

"Dad, you didn't like Reva either."

"I like her better than that thang that just left up out of here. At least Reva knew her got damn place. That little bitch needs some home training." He huffed. "You need to drop this woman and go and make things right with your wife. No need in you taking care of a woman who acts like she don't need you."

"You shouldn't be worried about any of that, Dad. All you should be worried about is getting better. I'll figure my life out soon enough." Adam sighed.

"Well I need you to get some urgency behind it. I won't be here forever."

Adam thought about what his father said. He and Reva got married when they were really young. She was what any man would want. She was obedient and submissive. Her goal in life was to love and please her man, something that Nixie knew nothing about. Adam just got bored with Reva.

When he met Nixie, she poured that fun and excitement back into his life. She was everything that he was missing until she wasn't. Now that things were so messed up with them, it had him in his feelings and wondering if he really did make a mistake.

Adam stayed there talking and making sure that his father was okay for the next couple hours, until the nurse came and told him that visiting hours for CCU were over. Reluctantly, he left the room and drove himself home with a lot on his mind.

The first thing being the fact that he never told Nixie that he was married before or that he was still in fact married. They weren't together for the moment, but on paper, he still belonged to Reva. He knew that Nixie wasn't going for that, so he had no plans on telling her.

Walking into the house, it was quiet, no music or loud cackling coming from Nixie on the phone. Adam dropped his things and headed upstairs to see if Nixie was at home. Her car was there, but she never liked for things to be that quiet.

When he reached the room, he had to stop where he stood. The sight before him had everything in him rising.

There she lay in a black sports bra and small cotton shorts that barely covered her pussy. She was lightly snoring, letting him know that she fell asleep right after a shower.

"Damn," Adam hissed. Nixie was beautiful to him, and he was still attracted to her despite their issues. It had been weeks since he was able to sample her greatness, and he wasn't about to miss this opportunity. If she was awake, he knew that she would more than likely turn him down, so he figured if he got her started and primed, then she wouldn't deny him.

"Ummm, baby." She mumbled in her sleep, and Adam smiled, thinking that she was dreaming about him, but that was the furthest thing from the truth.

"I got you, Nix." He smirked as he lowered himself and slid her thin cotton shorts to the side and ran his tongue the length of her slit. She squirmed under him and released a soft moan. Adam made small circles around her clit before he pulled her into his mouth.

"Shhhh, shit, baby, fuck!" She arched her back, feeding him more of her, and Adam obliged.

Eating pussy wasn't his strong suit, and it wasn't something that he normally did, but after the way his father talked to Nix and seeing the look in her eyes, it was the least he could do, on top of the fact that he hoped that it would end with him buried deep within her core.

"Shit, Airy, baby, suck hard. What are you doing?" Nixie rolled her hips upward. "Come on, Airy, eat this pu..." Nixie's eyes popped open, and she looked around the room, realizing that she was in her home. She jumped back, attempting to cover herself with a cover. "What the fuck, Adam!" She screamed.

The last thing she remembered doing was showering, talking to Airy, and then lying back on the bed. Airy absorbed in her thoughts as she drifted off to sleep. So when she felt the sensation of someone, her mind made her think it was Airy. Seeing that it wasn't had her feeling guilty and dirty.

"So you are fucking him?"

"Why the fuck would you do that, and I'm sleep?" Nixie's eyes were knitted together, and her tone was laced with rage. She was pissed and felt violated in a sense.

"Because you're my woman, I should be able to touch you when the fuck I want to."

"That's where you got shit twisted. Just because we were together doesn't mean that I'm your property. I don't belong to you. My body is mine, and unless I consent, don't fucking touch me."

"Were?" Adam said, standing up and heading to the bathroom to rid himself of her heavenly scent. He hated how good she smelt and the feeling that he was getting from pleasuring her. At least until he heard her call him by his boss's name.

"What?"

"You heard what I said, Nix. You said we were together." Adam stuck his head out of the bathroom. He was working overtime trying to control his anger, but he could feel it coming to a head. "And you called me Airy," he said when he came face to face with her again. "You're fucking him? Do you know what the fuck that will do to my career?"

"Adam—"

"No, fuck that." He slammed his hand on the dresser that he was standing near.

"You need to calm the fuck down." Nixie stood up so she could go clean herself off, but before she could make it by Adam, he grabbed her arm tighter than she could handle. "Let me go. You're hurting me," she growled through gritted teeth.

"If you weren't such a whore, I would give a fuck how you feel." He snatched her toward him and peered down into her eyes. "How would you like it if I were to go and fuck my wife?" he blurted out in anger.

Adam watched as the look on Nixie's face went from pained to angry in a matter of seconds. She cocked back and slapped the shit out of him, hard enough that he hurried and let her go and grabbed his eyes.

"You son of a bitch! You're married!" she screamed, picking up the lamp that was on the dresser and throwing it his way, causing him to have to duck to get away from it. "I knew your ass was a liar. I'm glad I fucked Airy, and I'm leaving your ass. Since your fucking daddy is the only one that takes care of you, take your dumb ass and go live with him. Better yet, go live with your wife. I can't believe you!"

"You are fucking my fucking boss. You don't have a leg to fucking stand on, Nixie. Fuck you."

"No, Adam, fuck you. I want you out of my house!"

"Put me out." Adam was not expecting things to go this way. He had plans on coming in and making things right until he figured out what he really wanted to do. Now she had drew his hand.

"I got somebody for that." She scoffed, snatched her phone, and walked in the bathroom, locking the door. "Muthafucka done lost his got damn mind." Nixie paced the bathroom, trying to get her emotions under control.

After realizing that was a task that she wouldn't be completing anytime soon, she hopped in the shower and cleaned Adam off her. She was disgusted and mad to say the least. She needed to get out of the house.

Once she was done with her hygiene, she walked to the closet and threw some clothes inside of her bag. What she didn't get, she would buy. She was leaving for a few days to give him time to get out of her house.

"Where the fuck do you think you're going? We need to talk about this."

"There ain't shit to talk about. We ain't happy. I stopped being happy a long time ago, and the fact that you're married was the push I needed to do the inevitable." She shook her head. "I will admit that it was fucked up to cheat on you with Airy, but I won't even lie. I never felt guilty about it, because I knew that we weren't meant to be, and it was only a matter of time before we ended. However, I should have ended shit with you way before I got involved with anyone else." She stopped and thought about things, and she did owe him an apology. "Despite you having a wife, I apologize for my part in shit, but that's it. I'm not sorry for anything else."

"Me and Reva have been split up. I left her for you. I didn't cheat on you."

"Nigga, you failed to tell me you were fucking married though! I'm nobody's side bitch or mistress. You can keep that bullshit, but like I said. The reason I even called you earlier was to tell you that we needed to talk, to end things, but when you told me about your dad, I felt like shit and kept my mouth closed. Now, I'm saying it. I don't want to be with you anymore, Adam. You want a woman who's gonna follow in behind you. That ain't me.

"I want to be free. I want a man that's okay with me being me and ain't scared of my growth. That ain't you, bruh." Nixie tossed her bag on her shoulder and tried to walk past Adam, but he pushed her back. "Yo, that's the last time you put hands on me," she warned.

"You think you get to just end things and go be a whore with Airy? You think I'm going to sit back and let that happen?" Adam released a sinister chuckle.

"Niggaaaaaa." Nixie ran her hands down her face before her gaze fell on him again. "You're married! You gotta a whole fucking wife. What I do is of none of your concern. Am I using this is an out, yep! Is that wrong? Maybe, but at the end of the day, we ain't meant to be, and no matter how we do it, it needs to be done. Goodbye, Adam. I want you out of my house, let's not get the police involved."

She tried to leave, and he grabbed her by the hair and pulled her back toward him, but Nixie wasn't going down like that. Thanks to the self-defense classes that she took with her mother and sister sometimes, she knew how to handle this. She turned so that he had to release her hair, and she raised her knee and kicked him in the balls. He folded, but Nixie wasn't done. She lifted her size seven and delivered a kick to the face, sending him to the ground and howling in pain. She then kicked and hit him until she was satisfied.

"I knew you were a bitch. If you not out of my house by tonight, you gon' hate the day you met me!"

With that, she opened the door and left him lying there withering in pain. The minute her butt hit the seat, the tears began to flow. She picked up her phone and dialed the one person she wanted the most at a time like this.

"What's up, baby? How did it go?"

"I need you!" she sniffled.

"What happened? Where the fuck are you? Did he hurt you? Talk to me, Nixie! Tell me something, baby. Hello!"

"I'm on my way to you." She struggled to not break down and make things worse, but it was hard. She couldn't believe that Adam turned out to be *that guy*. He was selfish, an asshole, narcissistic even, but a married woman beater, never in a million years. She was pissed at herself for not seeing that, and she promised herself in that moment that she wouldn't be that *blind* again.

Chapter Twelve

LESSON 12

Love Isn't Fair.

W hen Nixie pulled up to Airy's home, he was already standing on the porch waiting for her. The frown sketched on his handsome face had her heart battering her rib cage. The one thing that she had figured out about him was the fact that he was passionate about things he cared about, and for some crazy reason, she became part of *things*.

Airy was pissed, partly because he didn't know if she was okay. Hearing her sound so broken and scared and not being able to do anything about it, had him boiling internally to the point where he didn't even give her a chance to get the car off good before he was in her face, inspecting every inch of her.

"Nix, what happened? You gotta talk to me, tell me what..." His words trailed off as she looked down at the mark on her arm that was already taking on a purplish tint. He bit down on his back teeth in an attempt to contain his anger.

"Wh-what the fuck happened to your arm? Did he do this to you?"

Nixie choked back her tears before throwing her head back and clamping her eyes shut tight. She didn't want to think about what had just happened. All she wanted to do was to go to sleep in Airy's arms and pretend that it never happened, at least for the night, because tomorrow, she planned to make sure that Adam was out of her house.

"Can we just go inside?"

Airy cleared his throat, clearly annoyed that she wasn't giving him what he needed to fuel the anger that was already brewing. It wasn't that he wanted to go looking for trouble, but he couldn't just sit back and *know* that someone did something to someone that he cared about.

"Yeah."

Nixie picked up on the aggravation in his tone and grabbed his arm as he stood to turn and walk away. When their eyes met, she pleaded with him silently. She didn't want to fight with him. She needed him to help her through the emotions that were running rampant through her.

"Please." She whined while tears slipped down her cheeks. Even though she kicked his ass, she was still a little shook up at what happened, more so because she wasn't expecting any of it.

Airy nodded and then helped her out of the car. They went in the house and went straight up to his bedroom where she stripped out of her clothes and slid between his sheets. Nothing was said, no eye contact was made. The one thing that Nixie needed was to feel close to Airy, and the scowl on his face caused her to keep her distance, so she settled for the next best thing, *his bed.*

Airy stood by and watched, emotions at an all-time high. There was so much he wanted to say, but her energy was off, and he didn't know how to take it. Taking a step in her direction, his steps halted when her eyes met his.

"Are you going to tell me what happened?" Airy's tone wasn't forceful, but it held concern, which settled her anxiety a bit.

Nixie closed her eyes tightly, knowing that she couldn't *not* talk about what happened after showing up at this man's house battered and bruised. She wasn't technically battered and bruised, but it was enough to raise red flags and have Airy's nose flaring like he was about to blow a gasket.

Sighing heavily, she pushed a curl that had fallen in her face away. Her loaded gaze fell on him as she opened her mouth to speak and then closed it again, giving herself a few more minutes to gather her thoughts.

"I was sleeping, dreaming about you, and I guess I said your name and he—ahh, let's just say he wasn't too happy about that." She chuckled nervously, purposely leaving out the part about him eating her out. That was another issue for another day, but right now, she was emotionally depleted and wasn't about to have that conversation.

"Okay..."

"Okay... We argued, and I told him that we needed to end things, that neither of us were happy, and hadn't been in a while. He then proceeds to tell me that he's married, and he should have never left his wife for me. I flipped out and told him I wanted him out of my house."

"That doesn't explain where the bruise on your arm came from."

"I went to walk away from him the first time, and he grabbed my arm and held it tightly so I couldn't move." She sighed.

"First time?"

"The second time, he pulled me by my hair, and I beat his ass. I'm not some defenseless, damsel in distress. I handled it, and I'm sure he'll keep his got damn hands to himself next time."

Nixie's tongue swept across her bottom lip before she pulled it between her teeth in an attempt to stop the tears that were trying to come.

"I never said that you were defenseless, but that's not the point. You should never have to worry about coming up against a man. Fuck that. I'm fucking his ass up." Airy spun around and snatched his key off the dresser. Nixie barely reached him before he reached the door.

"Please! I *need* you right now. Fuck him. By the time he's be able to get up off that floor, he'll remember to never fuck with me again." Nixie's eyes searched Airy's. She didn't want to bring him into her bullshit. "*Right now,* I just want you to wrap your arms around me and make me forget."

"Nixie, that won't fix—"

"I *need* it... I need you." Tears raced down her face as she pleaded with her eyes for him to stay.

Airy was a man before he was anything, and knowing that another man put his hands on her had him infuriated. He wanted to do something about it. He wanted to make Adam hurt like he made Nixie hurt, but she *needed* him. His heart wouldn't let him let her down, but his mind and ego were fighting for the chance to protect her honor. It was a battle, and the only thing that made him somewhat relax was the fact he knew exactly where Adam worked.

"You're not going back to that house by yourself. I'll call Kawan to go and help me clear his shit out, change the locks and all that shit, but you're not going alone." Nixie nodded, not in the mood to go back and forth with him. She was not about to let Adam dictate her life and how she moved, but if it made Airy feel better in this moment, she would give him that. "Don't just agree so I'll shut up about it either. I'm serious, Nixie. It could have been worse."

"I know," she sighed and rolled on to her back. "Today was both emotionally and physically taxing, and I just want peace. You are my peace, Airy, my safe haven. Can I have that? Can I have you?" Her eyes cast down the length of his body before they found his again.

She had never wanted to feel a connection as bad as she wanted to in this moment. It was like her body craved him, yearned for him, and couldn't survive without *him*. She could see the rage that pierced through his orbs settle slightly as he focused on her small delicate hands that found their way to her nipples.

"Damn." Airy hissed as his hand moved over his growing dick. He shook his head because Nixie knew exactly what she was doing. She was his weakness, and her body was his playground. He couldn't deny it. He couldn't deny her.

Slowly making his way to her, he leaned down so that his hands were on the bed. He pushed her legs apart so that he was face to face with her pussy. The soft flowery smell coming from her middle had him salivating.

"No!" Nixie moved away from him as guilt rippled through her heart. Airy noticed her change in demeanor just as quickly as it happened and had a frown etched on his chocolate face. He went to say something, but instead, Nixie pressed her mouth against his.

When he tried to pull away, she grabbed the back of his neck and brought him closer, lowly moaning. Her small hands made their way to the button of his navy-blue slacks and tore them open, slipping her hands inside of his pants.

"Nixie—"

"I just want to feel you inside me... Can I have that?"

Airy grumbled and mumbled a few obscenities under his breath at the fact that Nixie knew for a fact that she could have anything when it came to him, and there was no need to question it. Even if it was to hide what was really going on with her.

"Whatever I have is yours. You know that."

Nixie's cheeks hiked at the same time a fresh batch of

tears fell down her face. Airy couldn't be real; there was no way that this man who had come into her life and made everything okay was really real, yet here he was.

Without saying another word, Nixie crashed her lips against his again, and this time, Airy took control. Parting her lips with his tongue, he worked himself the rest of the way out of his pants, stepping out of them quickly and slinging them from under his feet.

Airy was annoyed that Adam put his hands on her, and there was nothing that he could do about it in the present moment. That mixed with the passion pouring through his veins for Nix had his emotions at an all-time high, and he was on a mission to release it all.

Grabbing her by the waist, he picked her up and laid her down on the bed before climbing between her legs, never breaking the kiss. He could feel the heat and moisture as his dick came in contact with her middle, making him harder than he thought he could get.

"Ummmmm!" They both moaned as he slowly slid into her, breaking the barrier of her heaven.

"Got damn it," Airy hissed, biting down on his back teeth to keep from moaning out like a bitch. The way her wetness engulfed him had him taking in sharp breaths to control his breathing. "I swear I could live in your pussy." He growled, cuffing her thighs in the crook of his arms and bringing them back so that he had more access to her.

He watched her wince in pain as he traveled the depths of her. The grimace was replaced with a look of pure ecstasy moments later, followed by the sweetest moan that Airy had ever heard.

Nixie threw her head back and welcomed the slow strokes Airy delivered, each one meaning something more than the one before. The connection, the feel, the sounds coming from the both of them were different and more intense. It was laced with passion and eagerness of what they wanted to be to each other.

"You make me feel so good, Airy. Shit!" she hissed. "I love this." Nixie parted her thighs, taking in more of him as he picked up the pace a little, winding his hips in a circular motion every time his dick disappeared into her core. "Sssssss." Nixie threw herself into Airy, attempting to match him stroke for stroke.

"I love this shit too," came from behind his clenched teeth as he thought about the words that he was saying versus what he was thinking.

Airy had started to fall in love with Nixie. How could he not; she was beautiful, funny, and smart as fuck. The way she went after what she wanted in life made him want to do better as a man. She lit something on fire inside of him. He didn't fight the feelings, and he didn't exactly ask for them either, but there they were, and he embraced it *internally*.

She's not ready for that part of me yet.

Nixie's eyes found his as he worked her core like the pro he was. The way he knew her body, every single crevice, and was sure to show just the right attention at the right time had her over the hills with him, more so than she, too, was willing to say out loud. So instead of speaking, she decided to show him.

Her fingers sank into his muscular back, bringing him closer to her. She wanted to feel as much of him as she could, and Airy wasn't one to disappoint. Crashing his lips against hers, Airy enjoyed the feel of her middle sucking him in like he belonged there, and he did. Nixie was home, and his dick had no objections.

———

The sun flickered through the small space in the curtains, causing Nixie to groan. Her eyes fluttered, in an attempt to keep them shut so that she wouldn't fully wake up. However, that attempt was interrupted by her blaring phone beside her.

She went to turn so that she could turn it off but stopped when dull aching between her legs stopped her sudden movements. Memories of the night before had her cheeks hiking up. Airy was a whole different animal. It was like they had broken into another realm of their relationship, and he wanted to explore as if it would somehow go away.

"What do you want?" Nixie groaned into the phone once she finally had her hands on it.

"Why the fuck didn't you call me?" Her icy tone floated through the phone, cutting the tension that Nixie didn't know surrounded them, like a knife. "You already know that me, Mommy, Kawan, and Stan would have been over there before that bitch ass nigga could have even raised his voice."

Nixie clinched her eyes tightly as the *other* part of last night came rushing back to her mental. She winced as she moved her arm that was decorated in a bluish-purple bruise. Shaking her head, she focused on the task at hand, which was an attempt to calm Navi down.

"Navi, it's okay. You already know I put the moves on him." Nixie giggled, but Navi saw nothing funny about the matter.

"I'm glad you think this shit is funny. If it wasn't for Airy calling Kawan this morning, then I wouldn't have known anything about it. They went over to your house, and Adam's hoe ass better be glad he got his shit and left because Kawan and Airy was on his ass."

Navi paced her living room floor. She was supposed to be headed to her boutique, but when she got the call that her sister had been attacked, she couldn't focus on that. So she called in her manager to intercept the packages that were on the way.

"What did you say?"

"You heard what I said. They should be on their way back, and don't you dare get mad at that man for stepping up in your honor. You can't be so independent that you forget to let him be there for you. You can't expect him not to want to do something about this shit, Nix. Airy is a real man, so you should have known he wouldn't back down."

"I just don't want anyone to be mixed up in my shit. He doesn't need to get into trouble, and neither does Kawan. Adam is a bitch and got his ass beat. Like I told Airy, I handled it. I just wish everyone would chill the fuck out and let it go. He's out of my house, and I'm here."

Navi sighed. "I get what you're saying, but that doesn't stop us from wanting to be there for you, Nix, so stop trying to fight us on it."

"I just need a mental break, but I have shit to do." Nixie pulled herself out of the bed, stretching, ignoring the soreness of her body. Airy took her through it last night but in a good way. She smiled at the thought. "On another fucked up note, did Airy tell you that nigga was married?"

The line went silent as Navi processed what her sister had just said. Out of everything that Kawan told her, he had conveniently left that part out. After clearing her throat, she stared at the phone before she spoke again.

"Come again."

"You heard me, hoe. In the middle of us arguing, he gon' yell out that he should have never left his wife for me. When I tell you steam was coming out of my head, girl, I was pissed the fuck off. Like had I known you had a wife, I would have never even entertained the thought of you. Like that shit hit a little different."

"Yeah, that's some bullshit."

"That explains when I asked him to add me to his insurance, he said that he couldn't. I never dwelled on it. I just thought he didn't want his premium to go up, but all along, his hoe ass had a wife. And now that I think about it, Senior was always throwing out some slick ass comments about how he made a mistake." Nixie thought back to the many times that she and Senior had gotten into it about her and Adam's relationship. The way he used to say that she was a mistake. At least that's what she thought, but now it was clear that he was talking about the fact that Airy had a wife. "I just want to beat his ass for that again."

"But why? This is your out. Even though your hoe ass cheated on that man with Airy's fine ass, now you don't have to feel bad about it," Navi said like she had just solved all of Nixie's problems.

"I take full accountability for what I did. Regardless of his skeletons, me cheating was wrong, and me not feeling bad about it makes that even worse, but I own my part. What's done is done, and I should've listened to Mommy. Had I known his ass was married, then it would have been over long ago." Nixie paused going back and forth with herself with whether she wanted to reveal her true feelings or not. Sighing, she thought, *what the hell.* "As bad as I don't want to admit it, the shit hurts a little."

"Hurt? Why?"

"Because at one point, I cared about him, even loved him."

"But that shit ended as quickly as it started. He didn't even care enough about you to tell you that you were a sister wife."

"Bitch." Nixie placed her hand on her head and shook it. "I was not a fucking sister wife."

"Oh, but you were, but I gotta go. Mommy is coming to your shop, just a heads up. I'll probably be with her."

"Navi, I said I'm fine."

"I know what you said, but until we lay eyes on you ourselves, none of that matters. So I'll see you later, hoe. Oh, and what's your sister wife's name? I want to stalk her on social media." Navi was serious, and Nixie knew it; so without saying anything, she just ended the call. She knew it wasn't the end of the conversation, but for now, she was done.

Nixie threw herself back on the bed and looked up into the ceiling. Her life had turned into a little mess right before her eyes. She had worked so hard to keep her life in order and make sure that things like this never happened, and yet it was happening right under her nose.

"Oh God, I'm going to hell." She jumped at the sound of someone at the door. She looked around the room unsure of what to do. At first, she was going to let them knock in hopes that they would just go away, but they showed no signs of letting up.

Sliding on one of Airy's shirts that swallowed her small frame, Nixie trekked to the front door. Standing on her tiptoes, she peeked out the peephole and observed an older woman who looked vaguely familiar. Opening the door, she smiled until a frown etched its way onto the older woman's face. Nixie opened her mouth to say something but was cut off by Airy's deep baritone.

"What the fuck are you doing here?" Anger yanked hard on him, overriding sense as he moved directly behind Constance, bringing her focus away from the beautiful brown-skinned woman to him.

Jealous rage poured through her pores as she watched the man she wanted, silently ensure that another woman was okay. It burned her up to see the love pouring from his eyes when they focused on the other woman and the hate that spewed from them when they landed on her. Constance swallowed hard.

"So, she is why you don't want me anymore?"

"No! We were over long before she ever took possession of my heart." Airy was talking to Constance, but his eyes were on Nixie whose eyes ballooned at the mention of her having his heart. "But you knew that already." His statement was loaded and possessed more than one meaning, each different for each of the ladies standing before him.

"Are you sure, because I was just riding your dick on your patio not too long ago."

Both women tilted their head to the side with brows knitted in. Airy's focus and attention was only on Nixie as he spoke. He wanted her to be certain that what Constance was doing was trying to put a wedge into what she knew was something real.

"Again, that was before my life changed for the *better.*" Airy's eyes cast down to Constance as he shook his head. Before he spoke again, a small smirk spread across his lips. "What you trying to do here, Constance, because the last time I saw you, when you pretended to be a client, I told you that you would never have me that way again. Not physically, not mentally, and damn sure not emotionally. If Nixie walks out of my life right now, I still wouldn't give you that. The minute you laid on that table and killed my seed, you killed any chance of me ever wanting anything to do with you."

Nixie gasped and placed her hands over her chest, gaining Constance's attention. The scowl on her face was almost comical. She searched her light brown eyes, and there was something really familiar about them, but Nixie couldn't put her finger on it.

"Airy, you know that I've got a son that just turned thirty. Hell, I just turned forty-six myself. What was I going to do with another baby? Huh? I panicked; don't you see that? But now I'm ready to give you what you want if you just give us another chance."

"I'm gonna give y'all a few minutes. I've got enough going on without having to deal with this." Nixie threw her hands up, and Airy quickly made his way around Constance to grab her and bring her to him. "Airy, go handle that!"

"*That* doesn't matter right now, Nix. You do. Fuck all of that shit, and none of it matters to me. The only thing that matters is that you're okay. I know what you went through yesterday is fucking with you, and *this* just adds to it, but we are gonna talk about it and get through whatever is going on in your pretty little head." He kissed the top of her head, and she closed her eyes. She could feel the tears well up, but she fought them away and sighed.

"I'm gonna go shower." She leaned up and kissed his lips. "Handle that." She rolled her eyes, bringing a deep rumble from his chest.

"Yes ma'am." He kissed her again, and she turned to walk

away. It wasn't until he couldn't see her anymore that he turned around and gave his attention to Constance's tear-stained face.

"You love her?"

"Constance, don't do this. We rocked, and it was dope until it wasn't. You made a decision for you, and I did the same. I'll never trust you, ever. Every time I look at you or touch you, my first mind will go to my baby that I'll never get to hold or that I'll never get to see because you were selfish. You never thought about me or us, only you, and now you have to live with that." Airy tucked his hands in his slacks while delivering a menacing stare. "And I have to live with the fact that I ever trusted you in the first place. Even though I have my doubts and insecurities, I'll make sure that that woman up there will never pay for your mistakes. Now if you will, leave and not come back."

"Airy, I—"

"Definitely not debate or conversation worthy." The look he was giving her sent a rush through her and chills down her spine. She was testing him, and she knew that her chances were running out. Constance nodded and turned to leave. "Constance... make this the last time you show up here or anywhere near me again."

She turned to walk away, and Airy closed and locked the door before taking the stairs two at a time. Once he was in his room, his orbs landed on Nixie who seemed to be lost in thought. He didn't say anything; he just sat there and watched as she picked at her nails while sitting Indian style in the center of his bed.

"So that's your ex?" Nixie said, not bothering to look up. "Interesting."

Another rumble rippled through his chest as he shook his head at the evident shade that Nixie had just thrown. He knew that his and Constance's relationship was unconventional, but he didn't feel like it was anyone else's relationship to understand. They were good until they weren't, and when they weren't, he ended it.

"Very." Airy shrugged and leaned against the dresser, never taking his eyes off of Nixie, even though she was purposely avoiding him.

"That's why y'all broke up, because she had an abortion?"

Sighing heavily, Airy ran his hand through his curly coils that sat on top of his head before giving his attention back to Nixie who was finally looking at him.

"When I met Constance, it was just supposed to be *fun*. No expectations and no real direction. We enjoyed one another, and the age difference really didn't matter to me. Things kinda just fell into place with our relationship, but I expressed to her that I wanted children, and I wanted to have kids, a family, just like the one I grew up in." Airy crossed his arms across his chest. "I knew that she had a son almost my age, but that didn't bother me. She was ready and willing to give me what I wanted, or so I thought."

"How did her son feel about that?" Nixie's eyes searched his. She knew that she knew Constance from somewhere, but she couldn't put her finger on it. Now things were starting to make sense to her.

"I couldn't tell you because I never met him. She doesn't talk about him and told me that she didn't raise him because of her career or something like that." He shrugged. "I just took it as she was embarrassed and was trying to work through the thoughts of dating a younger man. It wasn't until I found out that she had an abortion that I knew that we would never work."

"She never wanted kids."

"Huh?" Airy uncrossed his legs and took a few steps in front of where Nixie was sitting, picking at her nails again.

"I knew that I knew her from somewhere, but the photo that Adam had was a lot older. She didn't look nearly as desperate as she did today." Airy's brows furrowed together as he tried to piece together what she was saying, but everything she said was confusing the hell out of him. "Constance, your ex, is Adam's mother. She left him when he was little because she wanted to chase her career. She's the reason he is the way he is today." Nixie chuckled angrily.

"Wh..." Airy ran his hands down his face as he processed the words that came out of her mouth. The phrase *it's a small world* could not have been truer in this moment. Crossing his arms back across his chest, he shook his head. "What the fuck, man."

"Yeah, my sentiments exactly."

"Look, this doesn't change anything for me whereas you are concerned." Airy made it to in front of Nixie quickly, taking her chin into his hands and raising her eyes so that they were focused on him. "That's our past. It has nothing to do with what we have going on."

"I know that, Airy. I'm just saying, this is a lot for anyone. All of it. Like, I'm definitely going to hell for fucking a married man. Now to find out that you're fucking his mother, it's all just a lot, and I don't know if I can or want to deal with it." That last part came out a little above a whisper as she nibbled on her bottom lip, bringing her gaze to his.

Oh fuck, I didn't mean that!

"*Was!* I was fucking her. I haven't touched Constance since the day that you came to my office. The things I felt for you after one meeting had my shit all fucked up, and I ended up making the biggest mistake of my life, by backtracking, but that was the last time. I have no secrets, and I have no reason to lie to you or anyone else. I've shown you how I felt and what I want, and that's you. The ball is in your court, Nix. How I move from this point on is on you."

His words came out a little harsher than he anticipated, but he couldn't help the feeling that what had just happened was going to fuck with what they had going on. His feelings for Nixie grew every time they spoke, touched, or saw each other, and the thought of not having that was pissing him off, especially since there was no reason in any of this affecting them.

"It's still a lot, Airy. I mean, I just found out that I wasted three years of my fucking life. You can't expect me to just throw myself into the fire again when I just suffered from third degree burns from the last time I trusted."

"I don't expect you to do shit but keep it real with me, Nixie." He released an exasperated breath and backed away from her and took his space back against the dresser.

Nixie squeezed her eyes shut; her emotions were taking her on a cruel ride. There was no *real* reason for her to be upset with Airy. Constance didn't weigh in on her situation with him one way or another, but she was taking her frustrations about what happened with Adam, out on him. It wasn't fair to either of them, but she couldn't stop the downward spiral in her head.

"Baby, I..." She stopped and sighed, shaking her head. "I just can't do *this* right now." When her eyes focused on him, aggravation mixed with something that looked like hurt, but she couldn't be sure because he shook it off soon after. "Just—"

"I'm gonna head out. Here are your new keys, and your alarm code is one-two-two-four. It's the very first day I ever laid eyes on you at your sister's Christmas Eve party."

"Airy, please—"

"At the time, I thought it was significant." He chuckled, but there was nothing humorous about it. "Damn, I feel like a bitch. It's women who usually create these relationships in their head based off of how they feel instead of what they're shown. I'm not real sure how the tables got turned, but they did and just... damn." He ran his hand down his face and chuckled again.

"Airy, that's not fair." Nixie shook her head as a fresh batch of tears fell down her face. "You know I was in a relationship when we first got together. I never lied to you."

It was true. Everything that she said was true, but he thought that maybe, just maybe, she felt a portion of what he felt. Hearing the uncertainty in her tone had him second guessing not only himself but his ability to see things for what they were. He was good at that, but Nixie had him off his square.

"You're more than welcome to stay here if you want, or you can leave...whatever *you* want to do. I'll holla at you later."

"That's not fair, Airy. All I'm saying is I need time to process this bullshit before I can think about what I'm building with you." Her tone elevated a few octaves, and it granted her an angry glare.

"Yeah, well love isn't fair, Nix."

Airy shook his head and left out of his room. The last thing he wanted was to fight with her, and he could tell that the conversation was about to take a turn for the worst. That, on top of the fact that he didn't quite know if he could handle rejection where she was concerned, he thought it was best that he just left.

His feelings for Nixie were more than he ever expected in such a short amount of time. He could see himself with her and raising kids, building a future. With all of that blurred, it left his feelings and emotions up in the air, and he didn't know if he could handle it.

Chapter Thirteen

LESSON 13

Love Requires Vulnerablility.

"Yo, yo' ass been walking around here like you lost your best friend. You canceling meetings at the last minute, you're not answering your phone." Kawan pointed down at his ringing phone.

Airy groaned and hit cancel for the thousandth time today. He wasn't in the mood to talk to anyone, not Nixie or his mother. The women in his life were starting to stress him out. The text message that came through let him know that his mother wasn't too happy with being declined, but he told himself he would just deal with it later.

"You need something?" Airy ran his hands down his face and sat back in his chair.

"I need to know what the fuck is eating Gilbert Grape, nigga. I just told you what the fuck I wanted. You ain't acting like ya self. You kinda acting like a...."

"A bitch."

"Yeah. I mean, I wasn't going to say that, but yeah, you showing some tendencies." Kawan chuckled, but Airy just stared off into space. "So what's up with it?"

"Nixie, man..." Airy dragged out as his hands found their way back down his face, and he shook his head. "Once I got back, Constance showed up—"

"Oh shit!" Kawan pulled up a chair and got comfortable in front of Airy. For the first time since he left his house, he laughed.

"Now who's acting like a bitch." He shook his head when Kawan flipped him off. "She stopped by on her bullshit, and Nix answered the door in one of my shirts, so you know that started some shit." Airy cleared his ringing phone once again and then leaned back in his chair. "The fucked-up part about that whole situation is the fact that she knows Constance."

"Nixie? How?"

"You ain't gone fucking believe this shit... She's Adam's mama."

"Yo..."

"Right, so that's where the issue came in. She started talking about how she didn't have time to deal with this right now, and she needed time to think. Said that she just found out that she just wasted three years of her life on a married man, and she didn't know if she could just open herself back up right now." Kawan didn't say anything; he just sat there and listened. "I'm all for that, but I wish I would have known she felt like that before I fell in love with her ass," he fumed.

Kawan went to say something, but his words got stuck in his throat, causing him to go into a fit of coughing. He furrowed his brows as he took in what Airy was saying. This was what he didn't want to happen and the main reason he tried to keep it from happening.

"Love, nigga? I told your ass to stay away from her. I know how easy it is to get caught up with a Land woman. Hell, Navi had me at *what's up, nigga*. I also know that when shit gets bad, it gets bad. Damn, man!"

Kawan was selfishly thinking about the argument that he was about to have with his wife. The two were extremely close, and the last thing he wanted was another man's issues in his home. They had enough of their own.

"I don't really want to hear that shit right now. I'm just trying to see where this shit is going with us. My fucking heart is already in it, and I thought hers was too."

"Listen, bruh, you gotta lighten up on sis. She just found out that she was in a relationship with a married man, and she didn't know. That's some fucked up shit to find out, even if you weren't all in the relationship anymore. She lived with that man, amongst other things." He gave Airy a knowing look, and he gritted his teeth at the thought. "I'm just saying, nigga, you already know what it was when you got with her."

"Nigga, I know all of that." Airy waved him off.

"So what's the issue?"

Airy thought about what Kawan said, and he was right. "Damn!"

"Yeah, nigga, damn. You all mad for no reason. Yeah, she

didn't say what you wanted to hear in that moment, but her head was more than likely all fucked up. You should have been there for her instead of adding more shit to an already fucked-up plate."

"Aight, man, I get it, damn." Airy frowned at Kawan, who flipped him off again.

"I'm just saying." Kawan shrugged and smirked at Airy who had his phone in his hand. "You ain't about to get her on the phone right now." He chuckled as he watched Airy's facial expression go from pissed to pleading in a matter of seconds. "You been ignoring her all day. She ain't about to fuck with you."

"Fuck, man!"

Airy hit the call button again to see if he could get her to answer. When she declined another call, like he had been doing all day, he grabbed his keys and jumped up from his seat. If she didn't want to talk to him, then he was going to make her.

"Fuck you going?"

"Nix Beauty."

Kawan ran his hand down his face, knowing that that was the wrong move, and he was making a decision to stay out of it. He was supposed to be meeting with Navi for a late lunch anyway, so he jumped up and walked behind him.

"I don't need a babysitter."

"Fuck you. I'm going to meet Navi for a late lunch. And I can bet my life that my wife is with her sister because you pissed her off and, in that instance, you're going to need me." Kawan smirked, and Airy nodded his head in agreement.

The minute the sun hit them in the face, Kawan cursed under his breath. As bad as he wanted to be the one to fuck Adam up for putting his hands on Nixie, he knew that this wasn't the time or place. Too bad for Adam, Airy didn't have that same mindset. Kawan knew that shit was about to hit the fan the minute Airy clenched his fist.

"So you like to hit women?" Airy bit down on his bottom lip, and the minute he was within reach, he swung so hard, connecting with the side of Adam's face, sending him stumbling back and eventually tripping and falling on the ground. "Huh, muthafucka? You can't hear now, bitch?"

Airy headed in his direction, but Kawan grabbed him, in an attempt to restrain him. Fighting his way out of Kawan's hold, Airy pushed him away when he noticed Adam getting off the ground. Swinging haymakers, Airy released every bit of pent up aggression that he felt.

Adam never had a chance. He wasn't much of a fighter to begin with, but the rage powered hits to his face and body wore him down a lot quicker than he would have liked.

"Airy, come on, man. What the fuck you doing? You got too much to lose right now." Kawan tried to reason with him, but Airy wasn't trying to hear it. "Look, man, he ain't even fighting back. Come on." Kawan grabbed Airy and pushed him back.

Airy went to swing until he saw who had hands on him. For a minute, he had blacked out and only saw blood. He remembered a time when he used to do that often, but as he got older, he learned to control it.

"Yo, chill!" Kawan barked when Airy attempted to charge Adam again.

"Muthafuckin pussy! You a hit a woman but you won't hit me. Get ya bitch ass up and do me like you did Nix. Grab on me like that." He tried to get around Kawan, but he couldn't.

"Nigga, chill the fuck out. People out here watching you," Kawan whispered harshly.

He looked out into the crowd and noticed that Navi was glaring at him with her phone to her ear. He was sure that she was calling Nixie, and sure enough, moments later, she came sprinting around the building that her shop was in.

"I'm trying to figure out why you mad though." Adam spit out a mouth full of blood as he grabbed his side and attempted to pull himself off the ground, to no avail. "Imagine my surprise while I'm eating my woman out and she calls out your name." He spit out another wad of blood.

Airy's whole body went stiff, and Kawan noticed it right away. Shit was about to go all the way left, and he knew it.

"What the hell is going on? Airy, you okay?" Nixie's typically soothing tone felt like needles piercing Airy's ears. The sound of her, the sight of her, even the thought of her made him sick in that moment.

"So yeah, I should be the one pissed. I spent three years with a whore." Adam chuckled through his pain.

"Adam, fuck you!" Nixie screamed.

"I tried that, but you were obviously thinking about my

fucking boss." Adam cringed when he saw Airy get close enough to kick him in the mouth. He groaned in pain as he shot a hateful look at Nixie. "You ain't even fucking worth it."

"That's one thing that I agree with you on," Airy said through clenched teeth. His loaded gaze fell on Nixie, whose eyes were stretched as far as they could go.

"Airy, baby, it's not like that," she pleaded.

Nixie went to Airy but stopped in her tracks when blue lights flooded the parking lot. Within seconds, the police jumped out and went right to Airy, placing him in handcuffs. It didn't take much for them to notice what happened, seeing Adam on the ground and Airy with blood all over his Italian loafers.

Nixie folded into her sister's arms as she cried her heart out. Things had gone from sugar to shit within a few hours. She knew that she should have told Airy what really happened, but what could she really say? *Adam ate me out while I was sleep, and I thought it was you until I realized it wasn't and stopped him.* Nixie knew that he would have never believed her.

"Nix, what the fuck?" Kawan asked, looking down at his sister-in-law who hadn't taken her eyes off of the police car that had Airy in the back.

"He hates me."

"He doesn't hate you. You lied to him."

"I didn't lie. I just didn't tell him *exactly* what happened."

"Omission is lying, no matter how you try and water it down. Do you know how fucked up it is to hear some shit like that about the woman you love? I don't know what the fuck I would have done if that were me. That kind of shit fucks with a man's mental, and now he has to sit on that in jail."

"He's not sitting anywhere; he'll be out shortly." Navi pulled her phone out. "Hey, Jacob," Navi said as she heard a chuckle on the other end of the phone.

"You mean Dad?"

"I wish the fuck I would call you dad."

"Why are you calling him? I don't need him for shit." Nixie tried to snatch the phone from Navi, but she stepped away.

"Yes the fuck we do, Nixie! *Jacob* is the only person that can fix this mess that *you* made. I don't want to deal with him either, but we *need* him, sis. So, unless you have a better idea, let me go have this conversation." Nixie looked from the cop car to her sister and then back to the cop car. When she didn't answer right away, Navi rolled her eyes. "Yo, Jacob, check this out..."

Nixie tuned her sister out as she watched the cop pull off. More tears flew down her face as realization hit her; this was all her fault. Everything that unfolded in this moment started and ended with her.

What did I do?

Just when Nixie felt a glimpse of happiness and something real, she found a way to fuck that up. She shook her head and covered her face with her hands and cried like she'd never cried before. It was at that moment that she realized just how much she really cared about Airy. She just prayed that it wasn't too late.

"Do you see what you've done!" Constance yelled as soon as she was in close enough proximity to Nixie. "This is why he dated more seasoned women. You young bitches don't do anything but play games. Now the love of my life is off in a police car."

Nixie slipped out of her slight depressed state and glanced over at Constance. When their eyes met, fury burned within her as she took a step in her direction. With everything happening, the last thing that Nixie had time for was a bitter ex invading her space unwarrantedly.

"If I'm not mistaken, you were told to steer the fuck clear from the both of us. Tuck your tail between your legs and take the L before I disrespect my elders and show you just how us young bitches do," Nixie fumed.

"Mom?" Constance heard from behind her. He thought that was her when she walked up, but hearing the words coming out of her mouth had him second guessing. "Ouch, shit." He flinched when the paramedic attempted to doctor on his wounds. He snatched away and tried to get down, but it felt like his body had been hit by a mac truck. "What the fuck are you doing here, and what are you talking about?"

"Adam?" She scrunched her eyes and then looked back and forth between him and Nixie.

It was then that she knew how she knew that young girl. She had seen pictures of her on her son's social media. She was kicking herself for not being more aware but it wasn't like she ever thought this would be an issue.

"Yeah, worry about the fact that *you've* been fucking your

son's boss!" Nixie yelled out. "Don't worry about me and what I do. Airy doesn't give a fuck about you, and he made that clear! I don't want to have to do you dirty, Grandma. Fall back."

"Mom, what is she talking about?" Adam hobbled over with his arm in a sling. "You're dealing with Airy too?"

"Was dealing with Airy!" Nixie corrected. "His heart belongs to me!"

"Well, this baby belongs to him." Constance placed her hand on her stomach and smirked. She was hoping to get under Nixie's skin and break down some of that confidence that lived in her heart, but the smile that spread across her face told a different story. She opened her mouth to say something, but Navi beat her to it.

"Pregnant!" Navi stepped up. "I know you fucking lying. What are you, like fifty? Bitch know her fertility died with Jesus! Don't listen to this shit, Nix."

"I am forty-six!" Constance stepped up.

"And your eggs are scrambled, smothered, covered, and chunked."

Constance's lighter skin turned a bright red before she mumbled a few things under her breath. Turning to her son, she looked at him with sorrow filled eyes. She hadn't done right by him, and she knew it, but there was no time to fix it now, and she didn't know if she wanted to. Marrying Senior was the worst thing she could have ever done, and from the looks of it, he was just like him.

She could tell by his demeanor and how he spoke to her

and Nixie. Her mind took a trip down memory lane for a second, she trembled at the memories of the verbal abuse she endured at the hands of the one person who was supposed to love her unconditionally. She couldn't imagine what her life would have been like if she stayed and she didn't want to.

"So, you left your family to come and chase a nigga that's my age? You fucked up my life so that you can be a whore?" Adam said, jerking away from the paramedic who was trying to get him back on the stretcher. "You are the reason I hate women so much; you are such a fucking shitty mother. I don't see what Senior ever saw in you." Adam shook his head. "As far as you," he turned to Nixie.

"Don't address her." Kawan stepped up and placed himself in between the two, itching to finish what Airy started.

"Nah, it's okay, Kawan." Nixie placed her hands on his chest. "Say what you got to say, and then after this, forget I ever existed."

"I actually feel sorry for Airy because he don't know what he's getting. My dad was right about you from the beginning. He said that you would show me soon enough that you were just like her." He chuckled angrily. "I hate that it took this to make me see, but I see. Whatever I left in your house, keep it, or throw it away. I'm done with you and anything that's associated with you. Fuck you, Nixie, and I hope he does you just like you did me." Venom laced his tone as she allowed his words to sink in.

Adam had allowed his mother to ruin his life enough. The horrible part of the whole thing was she didn't even care at the end of the day, so from that moment on, he chose not to care either. Hopping on the stretcher, he allowed them to get him situated to load him up on the gurney.

He was done with the women in his life and all that surrounded them. He was already mentally making plans with his wife who lived in South Carolina. A new start would definitely do him some good. There was no way that he could show his face at work again, and he didn't plan to, and he blamed Nixie for all of it.

"Hold on!" Nixie yelled, and she walked a little closer. "I'm sorry for cheating on you. No matter how shitty of a boyfriend you were, you didn't deserve that, and for that, I'm sorry. I take full responsibility for my part, and I forgive you for yours."

"You can keep that apology, and I had no plans on offering one. As far as I'm concerned, we were even. I had a wife, and you wanted to be a whore."

Nixie bit down on her back teeth to keep from spazzing. Things were bad enough, so she thought it better to leave the hostility out of it.

"I should have left you long ago, and that was on me thinking that you would learn to love me the way I wanted. That never happened though, and that was a *Love Lesson* that I needed. You were who you were. I shouldn't have expected you to change for me. I know that now, and I pray that I never come across it again." She turned to walk away but stopped and turned to Adam's angry glare. "That apology and forgiveness wasn't for you; it was for me. I'll be damned if I carry the baggage of what we had around with me. My future is far too bright for that bullshit." She winked and made her way back up the hill and to her shop.

"Sis, you okay?"

"No, I'm not, but I will be." Nixie sighed and wiped the lone tear that fell from her eyes. "Did Jacob come through?"

"Yes, but he said that he couldn't have his name attached because of his position, so he had a friend do it. Airy will be out as soon as he's processed, and the case will go away just like everything else that Jacob Land doesn't want to deal with." Navi chuckled. "I'm so glad that we came out on top without him." She looked over at her sister. "He does come in handy for something." She shrugged.

"As long as he doesn't expect a conversation or anything in return, because I'm happy without him."

"Nope. He didn't even ask how we were. Just asked what we needed and said he'll handle it. He's the same piece of shit he was when his little sperm slid up in Mama."

"Navi, I can do without the visual." Nixie rolled her eyes.

"I'm just saying." Navi giggled before clearing her throat. "So, what you gon' do about Airy? You gon' be there when they let him out?"

Nixie had been thinking about that from the moment he pulled off in the police car, and she honestly didn't know. She wanted to be there to explain to him what happened, but she couldn't take the look that was in his eyes. He had only ever looked at her with love and admiration, and to think that he thought anything else had her heart ripping in her chest.

"We both got shit to deal with right now."

"You can help each other deal with it. Don't throw away your forever on a technicality. Airy loves you, and even if you don't want to say it out loud, you love that man too. Don't fuck up your happy, Nix." Navi hugged her sister and allowed the soft sobs slipping from her mouth to fall onto her shoulder.

"He hates me, Navi. I saw it in his eyes. I can't take that. I want to fix it so bad, but I don't know if I can."

"You better before the Virgin Mary out there try and claim him. Homegirl is parched." Navi rolled her eyes, sending Nixie into a fit of laughter. "Please tell me that you don't believe that shit about her being pregnant?"

"She killed a baby of his before because she didn't want any more kids. Hell, she doesn't even take care of the one she has. So no, I don't believe it; she's desperate right now."

"I still can't believe that's Adam's deadbeat mama. I should have smacked one of the coats of makeup off of her face so I can really see what she looked like under there. Her body is dope as fuck though. Can't hate on the old hag."

"Navi."

"What, shit! I'm just trying to lighten the mood a bit. I know this has been a fucked-up couple days all around."

"I know, and I love you for it. I'm just gonna throw myself into work for the next couple days and get my thoughts together. I got my grand opening coming, and I ain't got no time to dwell." She sighed and ran her hands through her hair. "All of this is my fault anyway. I should have listened to Mom.

I was so busy wrapped up in Airy and not wanting to hurt Adam's feelings that I let all this shit linger on way too long, and it backfired. If Airy wants nothing to do with me, I don't blame him."

"You sound confused as hell right now."

"That's because I am. I just want to sort my thoughts and get everything ready for my grand opening."

"Humph! I'll take that as my cue to bounce then. I got shit to do anyway, hoe." Navi rolled her eyes and snatched her purse.

"Don't be like that, Navi. I just need to think." Nixie offered up a sympathetic smile.

"Yeah, whatever. I'll be back after my store closes to check on you."

"That works." Nixie waved and watched her sister walk out of the store.

The minute she was alone, she locked her doors and went straight back to her office and allowed her tears to flow freely. She missed Airy already, and the look that he gave her before he pulled away plagued her mind, and she couldn't not think about it. It killed her to know that what they had could possibly be over. Nixie knew she couldn't let that happen thought. She *needed* Airy.

"I do love him," she finally admitted freely.

Chapter Fourteen

LESSON 14

Love Means Letting Go Of Expectations.

Airy placed his back against the cold cement wall. His knees were pulled up to his chest, and his arms rested loosely on top of them. Pissed was an understatement. No, they weren't together, but she asked for transparency, so he expected the same thing in return.

So many things were flashing through his mind that it felt like he was going to go crazy. Now he knew why she didn't want him to go down on her the night before; she had already had her fix.

"What the fuck did I get myself into?"

"Must be women problems," the older gentleman that sat beside Airy on the bench in the holding cell said.

Airy turned slightly so that he could get a good look at the person who decided to invade his thoughts without his permission. He wasn't really in the mood to hold a conversation, but something about the older gentleman gave off a welcoming feel, but Airy didn't want that. Right now, he wanted to wallow in his own pity and think of how he could get Nixie out of his system.

"Yep, I know that look. Women are the only creatures that can bring out the pain and the anger at the same time." A hearty chuckle vibrated through his thick lips, bringing Airy's angry scowl to him.

His salt and pepper dreads were pulled up into a freshly twisted masculine bun on top of his head. A thin mustache lined his lips and dipped off on the side of his mouth into a neatly trimmed goatee. His eyes oozed wisdom but Airy's pride wouldn't allow him to receive anything other than silence. So instead of engaging, he just turned, dropped his head on his knees and sighed heavily.

"Let me tell you a little about women—"

"I'd rather you not." Airy glared at the old man who chuckled at the hostility. He had been where Airy was, so he didn't take the misplaced energy to heart. "I just want to sit here and be pissed. I don't need a jailhouse lecture. I already know where I fucked up. I should have never fucking opened my heart without knowing if she was worthy. Kawan warned my ass, and I didn't listen. So I already know what the fuck I need to do, so just let me sit here and figure out how to do that shit, aight?"

"Woooo, she must have really pissed you off," Frank said while slapping his knee and laughing. "I'm Frank, by the way, not that you care one way or another, but I figured it would be rude not to tell you."

Airy groaned under his breath. He hoped like hell that his father got here soon because if not, he could feel himself catching another charge.

"Let me tell ya a little something something. Women are complicated as fuck, but when you figure them out, it's the best feeling in the world. My Nonie was as mean as a firecracker. She gave me pure hell while I was courting her. It didn't help that I took her from her boyfriend." Frank chuckled, bringing Airy's eyes to him. "Yeah, she was with this man who wasn't no good for her. I told her as much too, but she was scared of the unknown." He held his hands out and wiggled his fingers to emphasize his point. "He was familiar to her. They had been together since high school, and then I came along five years later, and she couldn't let go of the time." Frank smiled and looked up to the sky.

Airy allowed his words to swirl around his head as he gave him more attention, turning his body slightly so that he was facing him. "So what happened?"

"Umph, I inserted myself into her life and didn't give her a choice about it. I knew that I was good for her, but she wouldn't allow her heart to make the decision for her, so I pushed. I made her choose."

"And she chose you?" Frank burst into laughter.

"I see you don't listen, youngblood. One of the first things I said was that women were complicated as fuck." He shook his head. "No, she didn't choose me. She told me that I expected something from her that didn't belong to me." He looked up at the sky again before his eyes cast down to the young man who was looking on in anticipation of what he was going to say next. "At the end of the day, her loyalty was to him. Yeah, we were going out and had even been physical, but she belonged to him. I had no right to expect her to show me some kind of loyalty when I hadn't even presented her with a commitment. When she said that to me, I got on my shit and was blessed with the best fifty years of my life." He laughed and clapped his large hands.

"Nah, if she's showing you that she cares about you and making you feel like shit is far more than what it really is, then she should be held accountable for that." Airy's brows dented in.

"Did you tell her that you wanted to be with her and only her? Did you give her the chance to make that decision, or did you assume because you were making love to her that she belonged to you?" Airy opened his mouth and then shut it as soon as he was done. "Exactly. Women like security and to feel safe. You were willing to sleep with another man's woman and hadn't even gave her the option of a commitment with you, and you wanted her to *trust* you with her? You young niggas are clueless."

"It's more to it than that. She fucked him."

"Did she tell you that?"

"No, she lied about it!"

"How do you know? Have you talked to her?" Airy grumbled under his breath before throwing his back against the cold concrete. "Exactly. You're taking the word of a man who was pissed off because more than likely his ego was bruised, thinking he lost his girl to another man. I'm sure he said whatever to piss you off, and you let him." Another fit of rumbles leapt from his thick lips. "Talk to her."

Frank was right, but the only issue with that was, he didn't *want* to talk to Nixie or see her. Just the thought of someone else between her thighs pissed him off to the point he knew he would say or do something that he would regret, so for now, he needed his space.

"Love is letting go of expectations. Stop expecting that she knew what you were feeling before you actually said it. If you want to be with her, tell her that, and then let her make the decision. Don't expect her to be a mind reader. And the expectation that she's perfect should have never even been a thought, because it will always leave you empty and disappointed. If it's worth it, if she's worth it, then fight like hell. If not, then don't." He shrugged and twisted his wedding ring around his finger. "But life is way too short to be anything but happy."

Airy nodded his head, taking in what the old man said without speaking on his true feelings. He was still in his head about the whole Nixie and Adam thing, and he was honestly tired of talking about it, so he chose not to speak.

"What you do to get you in here anyway? I never asked." Frank looked down at Airy, sensing trouble still brewing in his mind.

"I beat Nixie's boyfriend's ass for putting his hands on her, but that was before I found out she was still fucking him. You?"

"When my Nonie left me, I got into gambling pretty bad. I have my good days and my bad days, but tonight was a bad day. I was playing, and luck wasn't on my side." He sighed heavily. "I had bet all that I had, and all I had left was my wedding ring. I had a good hand and thought my luck was looking better. When I saw that I had lost, I felt like I was about to die. I pulled off my ring and was about to slide it over into the winnings pot when I realized the muthafucka was cheating. So I beat his got damn ass, sent him right to the hospital. I sure did. But I was more pissed with myself than anything."

"Why?"

"Because I almost lost the last thing that I had that reminded me of my sweet Nonie, all because I didn't want to lose. I almost lost everything." He held up his ring finger before bringing it to his lips and kissing it. "All because of pride and my ego. It's never worth it, son. Just think about that."

"Menz! Bail has been posted!" The corrections officer yelled as she opened the cell for Airy to walk through.

"Aye, Frank!" The older man opened his eyes and focused on Airy. "Can I post your bail or something? Give you a ride home?"

"Nah, I'm good. Stay up, youngblood." He nodded his head before he tucked his chin in his chest and closed his eyes.

Airy stood there looking at the old man for a while before he headed over to the where the officer was standing. Once she closed the gate, she escorted him to the front where he stopped when he got the clerk to gather his things.

"I would like to post bail for the gentleman that was in there with me." Airy looked at the officer who was clearly attracted to him. The way she dragged her tongue across her lips and eyed him up and down was a clear indication, and she wasn't trying to hide it either. "Ma'am," Airy said, jerking her from her nasty thoughts.

"Who, Frank?" She pointed to the direction that they had just left from. Airy nodded. "He doesn't want to be released. You see, when his wife died, he lost everything gambling. He's homeless, and when he doesn't want to sleep on the streets, he does something to get himself thrown in here. We like him, so we usually let him hang out for a few days unless we get crowded." She shrugged.

Airy's brows knitted in. He looked past the officer and then turned to the clerk who nodded his head in agreement to what was just said.

"Damn." Airy shook his head and thought about the conversation that he had with the old man. Love was a bitch, to make you want to give up everything because you don't have the one you love. He wanted to feel sorry for Frank, but the way he spoke made Airy feel like he was content with where he was, and throwing pity or sympathy on him just seemed wrong. "Thank you," Airy threw out before he went to head for the door, but the officer grabbed his hand.

He looked down at where her hand was and then back at her. The look he delivered told her that the thoughts that were traveling through her head didn't match the ones in his. To avoid the embarrassment of being rejected, she just let him go.

Airy released a chuckle as he made his way out of the building and soon after out of the door. It had been a long ass day, and all he wanted to do was sleep.

———

Bang! Bang! Bang! Airy groaned as he rolled over and looked at the clock that read 8:07 a.m. He shut his eyes tight, hoping that whoever was at the door would eventually go away. It had been two days since the incident with Nixie, and he had shut himself off to the world. He hadn't spoken to anyone, and he didn't want to. He just needed to get his mental to a balanced state before he presented it to the world again.

The person on the other side of the door, who he was assuming was his mother, wasn't about to let that happen. Reluctantly, Airy threw his legs over the bed and dragged himself to his feet. He felt like a lovesick puppy with Nixie, and it was starting to piss him off.

There wasn't a woman that was walking this earth that could make him feel the way he felt right now. That was how he knew that his feelings for her were real. She plagued his thoughts, his dreams, and almost every waking moment.

His emotions were scattered and all over the place; getting

a grasp on them were like trying to pull teeth, so he just let them run rampant. He missed her, and there was no mistaken it.

"Airy Montrez Menz, if you don't open this door right now, I'm gone kick it in!" Anna yelled from the other side of the door. Frustration and annoyance laced every word that poured from her perfectly pouty lips. "Open the damn door!"

"Enough hiding, son!" Airy heard his father's deep baritone seep through the door, and he knew he was in trouble. If his mother had solicited his father to come along, then there was no not opening the door.

With his hand on the door, Airy slowly turned the knob and pulled it open. When he came face to face with his parents, he knew that they were pissed. His mother placed her hand on his chest and pushed him back into the house, and his father followed.

"Have you lost your damn mind?" Anna started in the minute the door was shut. "We've been worried sick about you. I wanted to come here two days ago, but your father advised against it. I don't like this," she waved her hands in the air, "whatever this is!"

"Morning, Mother, Pops." Airy gave a head nod and then headed to his kitchen to fix some coffee. He definitely needed it.

"Don't get cute with me, boy." Anna followed while his father took a seat on one of the stools near the breakfast nook. "Now, what the hell is going on? That damn crazy girl calling me talking about she's pregnant and that you attacked her son because you slept with his girlfriend and that the little girl was trying to ruin your life."

"Wait, what?"

"And then you call us from jail of all places! We tried to come and get you and was told that you were already released, and all charges were dropped. The way they talked, it was like nothing ever happened, but there is video of you beating the shit out of an *employee,* of all people, and then getting hauled off to jail. I need you to tell me what the hell is going on." Anna threw her hands up and let them fall by her side.

"Hold on, y'all didn't get me out?"

"No, but I called my contacts at the station and they said that City Counselman Jacob Land told them to let it go; get rid of the paperwork." Arnez finally spoke up.

"You didn't tell me that, Arnez."

"Honey, when you're angry, you don't really let anyone say anything, let alone tell you something." Her angry gaze fell on her husband, who shrugged his shoulders and turned his attention to his son.

"Land?"

"Yeah. Police Chief called me this morning." Arnez nodded his head, and he scrolled through his messages to make sure that he indeed had the right name. When it was confirmed, he nodded his head.

"Who is that?"

"I'm not sure, but I'm sure it's someone close to Nixie. Her last name is Land."

"Nixie? Is this the woman that got you fighting in the

middle of the street like some hoodlum?" Anna placed her hands on her hips. "I thought she was *the one?*"

"She is... was... I—"

"How is she the one when she's got you out here ready to risk it all?" Anna's brows dipped in as she waited on her son to speak. He sighed before running his hands down his face.

"I hit him because he put his hands on her."

"Oh! Well you should have beat him down then." Anna rolled her eyes and took a seat beside her husband, letting her guard down just a little. She hated a man that puts their hands on women. She grew up in an abusive home and vowed to never be that girl or sit back and watch it happen to someone else. "So what the hell was Constance talking about, and that girl bet not be pregnant, or I'm beating your ass." She pointed at him.

"Constance is not pregnant, Ma. That I can promise you. She popped up at my house and saw Nixie there, and this is her way to try and insert herself in our shit. I've told her that there was nothing between us anymore, and she can't seem to let that go."

"I told you to let me beat her ass a long time ago."

"You always trying to beat someone's ass." Arnez cut his eyes at his wife. For the most part, he let her do and say what she wanted and just had her back if need be. But when it came to something that could put her life or freedom in danger, he drew the line when he could. "I knew that girl was gonna be trouble when you introduced us."

"Yeah, and when you broke up with her, she started doing

all that crazy stuff. Her ass is too old to be acting like this," Anna fussed. "Tell us about Nixie and why you don't know if she's the one."

"Some things went down."

"Things like what?"

"Anna."

"What, Arnez? I just want to know what woman got my son out here looking and doing bad. He looks like a lovesick puppy, and if I can help, I will."

"I thought you came here to kick his ass."

"I did, but now I feel sorry for him. You just said that he won't have a record. Yeah, we'll have damage control at the firm but nothing *he* can't handle. Plus, he reassured me that Constance wasn't pregnant, so we're good. *For now.*"

Airy and his father shook their heads. Anna thought she ran everything, and, in a sense and to a degree, she did. When either of them felt like she was doing too much, they would reel her in, but for the most part, they let her have her way. She was spoiled, growing up in a house full of men, so it was their fault.

"Nixie's ex is Constance's son, and we had a little disagreement when he found out that she *wanted* me and broke things off with him."

"Was that before or after you slept with her?" Anna narrowed her eyes, making Airy shift his body to the other side and clear his throat. "You don't even have to say it. I already know the answer. You got involved with a woman that was already in a relationship."

"She wasn't happy. He didn't even support her dreams. Dude worked at a real estate firm and never thought to say hey, let me help you find a storefront. He tried to stifle her potential with his insecurities, and she was miserable because of it. When I met her, I had no plans on doing anything outside of helping her, but the minute our eyes connected, I knew that she was something special. The more I got to know her, the more I fell in love. She was perfect."

"Was?"

"Some things came out that I wasn't expecting nor was I happy about." Airy crossed his arms over his chest. He had always been open with his parents, so speaking freely didn't really bother him. "You see, when I look at love and relationships, I measure them by you guys' success. Y'all are the epitome of marriage goals, and I want that one day."

Anna and Arnez both looked at each other before they burst out laughing. Shaking her head, Anna looked at her son with a smirk on her face. He had no idea what they had been through to get to where they are.

"Son, we," she motioned back and forth between her and her husband, "are not perfect. We fuss and we fight just like the next couple. With love, it's not *that* you fight or have problems, son; it's how you handle the turbulence." She shook her head again. "A relationship without problems is one with a ton of secrets."

"Yeah, fighting is actually not a bad thing as long as you fight effectively. It's all about how you fight," Arnez interjected.

"Airy, baby, you also have got to stop placing these expectations on people. You want your woman to mirror the one that raised you, and, son, that will never happen." Her soft tone was soothing, and Airy absorbed every word.

"What's so wrong with that? You're an amazing wife and mother. Who wouldn't want to attach themselves to that? The woman I spend forever with, I want to make me happy, like you make Dad happy, and raise my kids to be just like me."

"What a spoiled and entitled man." Anna gave her son the side eyes, causing Arnez to chuckle under his breath. "You're spoiled, Airy. You think things should go how you want them in your mind, and the minute it doesn't, you're ready to wash your hands with it."

"Ma, it's—"

"No, I'm not done. Even with that Constance, God knows I can't stand her guts, but you expected that woman to have a baby with you. From what you told me, she checked off all of the other boxes that you had, right?" Airy nodded. "But the one thing she didn't want to do, you threw her away, and you're doing the same thing with your *one.*"

"Ma, Constance let me get her pregnant and then killed the baby behind my back. There was no coming back from that. I told her what I wanted, and she agreed."

"But did you ever ask her what she wanted, or did you just lay down the law?" Anna waited for an answer that she was never gonna get. "So what did Nixie not give you that you wanted?"

"Her loyalty." Again, Anna and Arnez looked at each other and burst out laughing.

"I'm trying to figure out what's so funny." Airy turned around and continued fixing his coffee.

"You, son. You were a known side dude. She didn't lie to you or hide the fact that she was in a relationship. Her loyalty was to the man she was committed to. You can't be mad." Arnez glared into his son's eyes.

"That's fucked up, Pops. I ain't no side nigga." Airy waved his dad off.

"Son, but you were." Arnez laughed, and for the first time in a few days, Airy laughed too.

"Damn, I guess I was, huh?" Airy continued to laugh as he thought about his actions in the last few days. "I been acting like a straight bitch too."

"Aye!" Anna warned.

"My bad, Ma, but it's the truth." He chuckled as he thought about his behavior. "I didn't even give her a chance to tell me what actually happened. I just told her to stay the fuck away from me."

"Sounds like you got some fixing to do."

"A conversation is in order." He nodded. "And then we'll go from there."

"Well I can't wait to meet her."

Chapter Fifteen

LESSON 15

Love Is Unconditional.

"Well isn't this a nice surprise." Constance smirked as she leaned against his door frame. Dragging her eyes the length of his sexiness, she didn't miss the nice bulge in his pants. "I can't tell you just how happy I am that you called me. I've missed you terribly." Her words rolled off of her tongue so seductively that Airy had to bite his bottom lip to keep from laughing.

"I'm sure that once this conversation is over, you won't feel the same."

Constance cleared her throat and clenched her purse, sashaying her hips through the living room. The last time she was at his home, he embarrassed her when she tried to go up the stairs, so this time, she waited for instructions.

"We're in here." Airy's voice was even and low but had a no-nonsense undertone that Constance didn't miss.

Turning on her heels, she strutted into the massive dining room that she'd had the pleasure of joining him in for a meal or two. When she reached the table, she took a seat near the one that he was standing by, being sure to swing her hips enough to come in contact with his dick.

A low rumble vibrated through his chest at her advances, from the way she walked to the way she was dressed. He had to give it to her, she just wouldn't give up, but he was done with the back and forth with her, and he wanted it to be over so he could move on with his life.

Granted, he was still pissed with Nixie, he had made it up in his mind that what they were building was worth the conversation that was going to happen sooner than later. Right now, there was one more door that needed to be closed.

"So, what do *I* owe the honor?" Constance purred as she ran her finger around the rim of her glass of water that was placed in front of her.

"Tequila Sunrise? It's your favorite." Airy smiled as he poured the Patrón in the glass, followed by the orange juice. Constance didn't really care for the grenadine so Airy lightly spooned it on so that it appeared to be the perfect sunset. Constance smiled at the fact that he remembered.

Sliding the drink over, Airy watched as she gave it a small shake then turned it up to her lips. She moaned as the flavors of the tequila and orange juice mixture did a small dance on her taste buds.

"No one makes these like you." She smiled as she placed the glass back down.

"Yeah, and no one lies like you." Airy peered down at Constance. "If you were *pregnant*, you wouldn't be consuming alcohol, now would you?" Airy searched her eyes. When they ballooned and then narrowed, he laughed. "Unless you were trying to kill another one of my babies."

"Airy, listen, I don't know how many times I can apologize for that. You keep punishing me for the same things over and over. What do you want me to do?"

"I want you to move on with your life, Constance. It doesn't matter what you do and say, everything I felt for you died on that operating table. That's just the reality of it."

"We can have another baby though. I'll do whatever you want me to do."

"Why, so you can leave it and me when you find something better to do?"

"Airy, that's not fair. You have no idea what my life was like with Senior. He was a mean son of a bitch, and if things weren't his way, then it was no way. I felt smothered like I couldn't breathe. I had to leave, but that doesn't mean I don't love my son. I just had to do what was best for me."

Constance took in a few sharp breaths before she let them out slowly. She hated thinking about her life with Senior because it was a time in her life where she was truly unhappy. He did any and everything to make her life hell. When she finally left, she felt more free than any bird in the sky, and she refused to ever go back to living like that.

"That's what I'm saying to you. I want a family, just like he did. I'm not going to be okay with you flying all over the world every other day. I want stability." Airy shrugged, not sorry about how he felt, and he could see the shift in Constance's eyes. "On top of all of that, I'll never forgive you for doing what you did. You really want to live like that? Always hearing about what you did wrong and what you couldn't get right? I know I don't. We would both be miserable; don't you see that?"

Tears welled up in her eyes because she never even thought about things like that. All she wanted was the vision that was in her head of what they could be, what they *were*. Sighing, she grabbed her glass and took a huge gulp from the cup.

"I just thought that—"

"That things could go back to when they were good?" She nodded. "That will never happen, because I will never forget what you took from me." Airy's honesty hit her like a ton of bricks. It wasn't like he hadn't said it before, but something about the conviction in his words really made it settle in her spirit. "You're so stuck on what could've been that you're not seeing what shit is right now, and none of it includes me and you."

"You must really love her."

"I do!" he admitted easily.

"But she cheated on you with my son. I watched the whole thing unfold. I was there to tell you that I was leaving. I got a job offer in California. I was kind of hoping that since everything went down that you would ask me to stay, but I see that's not the case."

"First off, Nixie didn't cheat on me, because we aren't together, but that's something that we will have to talk about. Second, even if we decided that we didn't want to focus on what we've built, I still wouldn't want to be with you."

Constance's eyes stretched at the realization that they were definitely over. There wasn't even a slither of hope. It was gonna take some self-talking to get a man like Airy out of her system, but she was starting to see that she couldn't force him to want her, just like Senior couldn't force her to be what she didn't want to be.

"I see." Constance grabbed the glass and picked it up and emptied the contents in one huge gulp. "There is no chance that we could ever—"

"None!" Airy cut off the thought before she had a chance to finish it.

"Well, I guess that's my cue to leave. My flight for California leaves tomorrow, and since there is no reason for me to stay here, I guess I'll be catching that flight."

"I think that's best, Constance."

Standing, she grabbed her purse and turned to head for the door. Airy reached around and held it open for her to walk through it.

"I should have known this wasn't a pleasant meeting; there was no food." They both shared a laugh. Constance looked up into Airy's eyes and caught a glimpse of what she fell for. "How about one last ride in the—"

"No, Constance." She rolled her eyes in the sky playfully.

"Fine!"

She placed her hand on his chest and leaned on her tiptoes and tried to kiss his lips, but he turned his head, and her lips landed on his cheek. She giggled and allowed her lips to linger just a second too long. Airy pulled back and tucked his hands in his ball shorts.

"Take care of yourself, Constance. I wish you nothing but the—"

"It be the muthafuckas asking for transparency that auras be murky as fuck!" Nixie yelled with her hands on her hips. The minute the smirk appeared on Constance's face, she went to lunge at her but was caught midair.

"Constance, don't even fucking try it. We just talked about this," Airy warned as she shook her head and headed for her car.

"I didn't even say anything."

"You didn't have to. I know you." Airy growled as he struggled to keep Nixie from getting to her as she walked past.

"Chill, little girl. He's all yours. I don't know what you did to him, but it worked. You won't have any more issues from me." Constance laughed and threw her hands up. "But, Airy, if it don't work out, look me up. Cali is a really nice place."

"Bitch." Nixie fought against Airy's hold as they watched Constance pull out of the driveway with a wave.

Once she was gone, Nixie jerked away with tears streaming down her face. She pushed Airy, who grabbed her arms and pulled her back to him.

"Is that what we're doing? Huh? Playing get back, Airy? Is

that what you do?" She screamed in his face with a scowl on her face. "Love doesn't keep score."

Nixie had tried her best to stay away from him, but it had proved to be harder than she ever thought. She felt lost and empty not being able to talk to him or see him. She needed to feel his presence to settle the uproar in her heart.

Putting her pride to the side, she got in her car and drove across town to see if he would talk to her. She was sweating bullets when she pulled up, but the minute she saw another car, her nerves turned to anger instantly.

"First off," Airy said before taking both sides of her face and shoving his tongue in her mouth, which she accepted immediately. The connection took both of their breaths away as he pulled her in more to deepen the kiss. When he pulled back, he searched her eyes.

"I didn't let him touch me willingly," she threw out, and when she saw his eyes turn dark, she grabbed his arms and made him look at her. "No, not like that. I fell asleep after I talked to you, and I was dreaming about us making love, and then I felt his mouth on me. But I thought I was still dreaming or maybe I thought it was you, so I moaned out your name. When I opened my eyes, I realized where I was at, and then I slid away from him as fast as I could. I felt guilty instantly because you had my heart. I felt like I was cheating on you, and that's when the fight started."

"Why didn't you tell me that when you got to the house?"

He believed what she was saying. He didn't know why, but it was something about her tone and the look in her eyes that said she was telling the truth, and it made him feel like more of an ass than he already felt.

"What the hell was I going to say? My boyfriend, who I was there to break up with, ate me out while I was sleep, but I thought it was you and I even called him your name." She rolled her eyes.

"That's what happened, right?"

"Yeah, but—"

"No buts. Transparency, remember? Always keep it real with me, and I'll do the same. No matter how it sounds or looks, I'll always take your word until you give me a reason not to, and I expect the same from you." Nixie nodded. "And I'm sorry too. I let my expectations put you in a box with how I wanted you in my life, and that's not fair. I want to be with you, but I understand that you need time to get over the shit that you went through with Adam."

"No! I was already one foot out the door before I even met you. The friendship and bond that we've built, I would be a fool not to explore it. You've been everything to me, even when I didn't deserve it. I want to do this, with you."

"Good, because I wasn't really gon' give you space, but I was going to pretend like I was." He smiled and pulled her to him and kissed her lips.

"Wow, Airy, just wow." Nixie laughed and then looked into his eyes. "Did you—"

"Nope. I fed her tequila to prove that she wasn't pregnant, and then I told her that I loved you, and anything that we had was in the past, and I was done with her bullshit. She's leaving for Cali in the morning, and I couldn't be happier."

"I love you too," Nixie said, tucking her bottom lip between her teeth. "With all of the L's I've taken when it came to love, I can feel it in my spirit that I finally got it right with you."

"There are never losses when it comes to love, only *Love Lessons*."

EPILOGUE

LOVE IS A CHOICE YOU MAKE EVERY SINGLE DAY.

"Shiiiitttttt." Nixie hissed at the sensation of his long, deep stroke, embedding her freshly manicured nails into his muscular back as he dove deeper, searching for something, anything to make their connection stronger. "Damn it, baby."

"Fuck! I love you, Nix," Airy said as he pushed her legs back further and buried his face into her neck to muffle the moans that were leaving his lips inadvertently.

"Baby, I love you too." Her eyes rolled back into her head. "God, this feels amazing."

Nixie arched her back to meet his thrusts, making him pick up speed while he released low hearty grunts. Wanting more of her, Airy lifted her hips and drove deeper, probing Nixie to cry out, and her legs began to shake.

Her orgasm rumbled in the pit of her belly as she succumbed to the pleasures of her sexual bliss. "Shit, I'm about to… oh shit, Airy. Yes, baby." She urged him to continue doing whatever he was doing that was throwing her core into an electrifying frenzy. "Oh my God, yesss." Nixie arched her back and released everything that Airy had built up.

"Fuck, Nix, you gon' make me nut." Airy took in a gulp of air to try and control his breathing. The tightness of her core had his breathing and heart rate out of control. As bad as he wanted to fight it, he couldn't, so he pumped a few more times and released into her waiting middle.

"Shit!" Nixie yelled as he stiffened inside of her. She ran her small hands up and down his back, making him shiver while he tried to get his bearings.

"I think your pussy gets better every time I enter it." Airy slowly pulled out, disappointed at the loss of connection but knew that it had to be done. "Fuck, I can't wait to get back home tonight."

Nixie giggled because since the day they finally made it official, they had been held up in the house, only coming out to go to her shop, and Airy had a few meetings that he had to go to, but for the most part, they had been attached at the hip.

Conversations flowed naturally, and they laid everything out on the table—feelings and concerns, wants and needs, and anything else that they could think that the other needed to know.

Airy was shocked at the story she told him about her father, but after hearing it, it explained a lot, and he respected her mother so much more. He was grateful for her father for handling his issue, but if he ever saw him, it wouldn't be a pleasant meeting. The fact that he hadn't even reached out to Nixie since helping was a shock to him. She explained that he does the bare minimum to not be considered a deadbeat, but in Airy's eyes, he was worse than a deadbeat. It was a good thing for Airy not to meet him because if he ever did, he would have a few choice words.

"I can't believe today is my grand opening."

"You've worked so damn hard, and I'm so damn proud of you. I can't wait to show you just how proud I am when we get back."

"You are so damn nasty." Nixie giggled and tried to get up out of the bed but stopped when she felt a faint aching feeling between her legs. She glared at Airy over her shoulder.

"What?"

"I'm a little sore, and now I'm gonna be walking all weird. You know you're not small. You should have taken it easy."

"My bad. You want me to kiss it?" He raised a brow, and Nixie smacked her lips.

"No. You *kissing it* is what got me into this mess." She giggled and moved out of his grasp when he tried to grab her. "No! Come on. We got to go set up."

Airy groaned as she got up and walked to the shower, trying his hardest to keep his hands to himself. His physical attraction mixed with the connection that he felt made it hard for him to keep his hands off of her. Whenever she was in his space, his hands had to touch her.

An hour later, they both were showered and dressed and

ready to go. The ride over, they talked about what they expected for the day, while Airy weaved in and out of traffic smoothly with one hand on the wheel and one hand intertwined with hers.

"Where the hell have y'all been?" Navi placed her hands on her hips. "You told me to be here at nine, and your fresh up off a fuck glowing face is thirty minutes late."

"Navi!" Natalia scolded and shook her head, and she walked over and hugged her daughter and then made her way to Airy. "I'm glad to see you here, and I'm still waiting on that family dinner."

"Actually, I wanted to get that planned soon. I'll get with my parents who will—ah, they're pulling up now."

Nixie squeezed Airy's hand and narrowed her eyes at him. He didn't tell her that his mother and father were coming early. She didn't know if she was prepared to meet them after everything that happened. They probably thought she was bad news.

"Relax." Airy leaned over and kissed her cheek, letting go of her hand to go over and greet his parents.

Nixie's fingers immediately went to her temples, and she rubbed them in a circular motion while mumbling under her breath. Nervous energy took over her body. Her eyes scanned their immediate area, looking for a way out.

"Where you think you going? You need to meet the in-laws." Navi laughed, grabbing her sister's arm, holding her in place.

"You gone make me fu—hey, how are you?" Nixie jerked

away from her sister and smiled at who she now knew as Airy's parents. She held out her hand to shake, but Anna knocked it down, causing Natalia to step up.

"I don't shake hands with family. We hug." Anna smiled and grabbed Nixie up. She melted into her embrace, and Natalia settled down where she was standing.

"Calm down, killa," Navi said to her mother who swung at her, hitting her in the shoulder. Nixie chuckled before pulling herself away from Anna.

"I see you don't play about your daughter," Anna said, taking a few steps toward Natalia. Her expression was neutral. There was no sign of confrontation, but Airy knew his mother, and Nixie knew hers.

"I don't." Natalia stepped up, and the two women had a short stare down before they broke into smiles. "Anna, I thought that was you. I ain't see you since you stopped getting your nails done at that place over there in Ballantyne." Natalia threw her arms around her.

"I know, and we never really switched numbers or anything like that, and when I stopped going, I tried to get Mimi to give you my number, but she was still pissed at me for acting up in the salon." Both women laughed.

"Do I even want to know what you did?" Arnez walked up and took Nixie into his embrace. "It's very nice to meet you, sweetheart. I'm excited my son fixed whatever y'all had going on because he was down in a bad way."

"Really, Pops?" Airy shot a pointed look at his father.

"Mr. Menz—"

"Don't you dare. You can call me Arnez or Pop, whatever you choose." His smile was infectious, and she couldn't help but to smile too.

"I just wanted to apologize for all that mess at your place of business. As a business owner, I know what that could do to your reputation and—"

"Nonsense. If a man puts his hands on a woman, he deserves to get his ass beat. Airy handled that, and everything is fine," Anna butted in, drawing a head shake from her husband. "I wanted to thank *you* for handling what could have been a life changing legal matter."

"Oh, no thanks needed. That's the least their deadbeat could have done." Natalia interjected and had Stan shaking his head.

"Well, looks like we're all gonna be one big happy family," Airy said as he threw his arms around Nixie and then leaned down and kissed the side of her face.

"I'm not complaining." Nixie shrugged.

"Me either," everyone said in unison before they all laughed and headed into the shop to set up for Nixie's grand opening.

A little while later, Kawan's parents showed up, and everyone got busy getting everything ready for later that day. Nixie stood back with tears in her eyes at the love that filled the room. Even with Airy's parents that she had just met, she got nothing but good vibes. If this was how life for her was going to be, she was in heaven.

"What you over here thinking about?" Airy stepped

behind her and wrapped his arms around her waist.

"This." She waved her hands around the room at everyone laughing and working. Her heart swelled, and she didn't know what to do with it.

"Well get used to it because I'm not letting you go. I've learned my lessons, and now it's time for me to use what I've learned and make you the happiest woman in the world."

"I got a few things I want to share that I've learned too." She turned around and wrapped her arms around his neck. "You want to know the biggest lesson I've learned through all of this?"

"What's that?"

"Love is a gift, one that I promise to cherish."

1 Corinthians 13:4-5: "Love is patient, love is kind. It does not envy, it does not boast, it is not proud. It does not dishonor others, it is not self-seeking, it is not easily angered, it keeps no record of wrongs."

YOU NEVER LOSE WHEN IT COMES TO LOVE, YOU ONLY LEARN... *LOVE LESSONS*!

The End

NAVI AND KAWAN'S STORY

UP NEXT

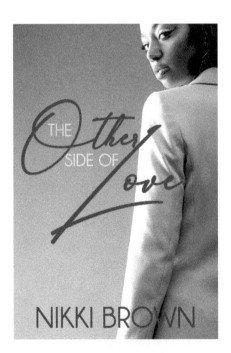

CPSIA information can be obtained
at www.ICGtesting.com
Printed in the USA
LVHW081752061120
670969LV00012B/1511